"I'm going to kiss you now," he whispered, seizing her in his arms. "Just act natural."

No! Jordana screamed, but the word got trapped inside her throat.

In a blink, she was in his arms, flat against his chest, experiencing the pleasure of his kiss for the first time. He didn't disappoint. He kissed her deeply, thoroughly, and with remarkable tenderness. Jordana didn't know what to do, but in typical Morretti fashion Dante took the reins.

Forgetting they had an audience, Jordana gave herself permission to live in the moment, to enjoy being in his arms, and his sensuous kiss.

Dante moved his lips against hers, took his time pleasing her with his tongue and mouth.

Goose bumps flooded her arms and zipped along her spine. His caress made her feel alive, oh-so-good, caused her body to throb with desire. He cupped her face in his hands, urged her to come closer. At his touch, her heart jumped for joy. He tasted sweet, like her favorite chocolate dessert, and she was hungry for more. *I can't believe it. This is* really *happening. Dante's kissing me and it's perfect, wonderful, the best kiss I've ever had.*

Dear Reader,

The idea for *Seduced by the Mogul* came to me while reading a titillating article about relationships in my favorite magazine. I've never written a friends-turned-lovers story but once I "met" Dante and Jordana, I knew they were a perfect match. I didn't realize *Seduced by the Mogul* would be filled with a dramatic, over-the-top proposal and erotic love scenes, but I should have known—after all, Dante *is* a Morretti.

In the dictionary, under the word *alpha male* should be a full-length picture of Dante Morretti. The real estate mogul is accustomed to calling the shots. But Jordana Sharpe, the Midwest beauty with the effervescent personality and fiery wit, is having none of it. Friendship be damned. It is high time Dante learned to compromise, because if he doesn't change his stubborn ways their fake marriage will be over before it even starts!

Writing Jordana and Dante's love story—a passionate, heartwarming tale about two friends who succumb to their desires and the will of their hearts—I was struck by how much Dante adores his son. Matteo is his world, and their incredible bond made me fall in love with them instantly. I hope you do, too.

Hearing from readers is the highlight of my day, so keep the messages coming! I appreciate you, and I'm humbled by your support. Happy reading.

All the best in life and love,

Pamela Yaye

Pamela Yaye

ISBN-13: 978-0-373-86442-3

Seduced by the Mogul

Printed in U.S.A.

Pamela Yaye has a bachelor's degree in Christian education. Her love for African-American fiction prompted her to pursue a career in writing romance. When she's not working on her latest novel, this busy wife, mother and teacher is watching basketball, cooking or planning her next vacation. Pamela lives in Alberta, Canada, with her gorgeous husband and adorable but mischievous son and daughter.

Books by Pamela Yaye

Harlequin Kimani Romance

Games of the Heart
Love on the Rocks
Pleasure for Two
Promises We Make
Escape to Paradise
Evidence of Desire
Passion by the Book
Designed by Desire
Seduced by the Playboy
Seduced by the CEO
Seduced by the Heir
Seduced by Mr. Right
Heat of Passion
Seduced by the Hero
Seduced by the Mogul

Visit the Author Profile page at Harlequin.com for more titles.

A special thanks to my bestie, Patrice Virtue.
Thank you for being the best friend a girl could ever have!
I appreciate you babysitting the kids so I could write
(and for treating them like your own), and for making me
all those delicious dinners, as well. One day soon,
I'll take you to a Toronto Raptors game so we can
cheer on *your* beloved team (courtside seats. I promise!).
One love, Patrice.

Chapter 1

The Bombardier Challenger 850 Learjet landed at Los Angeles International Airport with such ease and precision, Dante Morretti didn't realize it was on the ground until he opened his eyes and looked outside the window. The sky was free of clouds, cobalt blue and awash with radiant sunshine. It was another warm, spring day in the City of Angels, and Dante was glad to be home. Though born in Venice, Italy, he loved Los Angeles and would never live anywhere else. Everything he'd ever wanted was in LA—fame, power, prestige. And he was there to stay. At twenty-eight, Dante had a life most men dreamed of, but it wasn't enough. He wanted greater success, more billionaire clients, and he wasn't afraid to work hard for it.

"I thought you might be thirsty, so I brought you some mineral water."

Turning away from the window, Dante regarded the stewardess. She had rosy cheeks and fiery-red hair, and she spoke with a Southern twang. Her black uniform revealed an obscene amount of cleavage, but she wore an innocent, good-girl smile.

"Is there anything *else* I can do for you?"

Dante dodged her lascivious gaze, instead pretending to stare at the flat-screen TV that was showing the local news. The stewardess had been throwing herself at him ever since he'd boarded his company's private jet fourteen hours earlier in Hong Kong. But Dante wasn't interested in joining the mile-high club. Did she read the article in *LA Business* magazine? *Is that why she's throwing herself at me? Because she wants to sink her teeth into my millions?*

As the jet crawled toward the terminal, his mind returned to the photo shoot he'd done three months earlier at his Beverly Hills bachelor pad. He'd given an exclusive sit-down interview to the magazine, and once the April issue had hit newsstands, Dante couldn't go anywhere without being recognized. Gold diggers propositioned him everywhere—at the gym, on street corners, in restaurants and cafés. The more he resisted them the more aggressive they were. And the only thing Dante hated more than a provocative woman was a cheating one. Like his ex-wife.

Slamming the brakes on his thoughts, he gave his head a hard shake and considered the events of the past week. The magazine article had shined a bright spotlight on The Brokerage Group. Founded in 1998 by three UCLA graduates, the LA-based company specialized in the acquisition, development and construction management of all property types, including shopping malls, condominiums, luxury hotels and office buildings. For five years, Dante had been the chief investment officer of the Fortune 500 company, and in spite of his furious work schedule, he loved his job. His undergraduate degrees in business management and urban planning had given him the necessary tools to excel in the field. He'd led his company to record profits each year and made it look easy.

Pride filled him, turning his frown into a broad smile. Celebrities, politicians and savvy investors from all across the country were eager to do business with The Brokerage Group, and Dante was the reason why. His private company, Morretti Realty & Investments, was making money hand over fist. Thanks to his brothers Emilio and Immanuel, and his cousins Demetri, Nicco and Raphael, his firm had grown by leaps and bounds in the past six years.

"Would you like a back rub? I've been told I'm great with my hands." She leaned against his seat and twirled a lock of hair around her index finger. "Among other things."

I'm not surprised. I bet you've massaged *every man you've ever met.*

"No, thank you—"

"You don't know what you're missing," she continued, in a singsong voice. Her eyes were glued to his crotch, and the expression on her face was pensive, as if she was cooking up mischief. "If you change your mind just give me a shout."

I won't, he thought. *Trust me. I know trouble when I see it, and you're it.*

The stewardess sashayed down the aisle, switched and swiveled her wide hips. Dante was glad to see her go. Women were a distraction he just didn't need, and even if he wanted female company—which he didn't—he wouldn't hook up with an aggressive redhead with dollar signs in her eyes. It would be someone elegant and classy, with a successful career and her own money. He was a real estate developer, not a bank. Dante was tired of women expecting gifts, jewelry and luxury cars from him. *Why can't I meet someone normal like...Jordana?*

At the thought of the Midwest beauty, a smile filled his face. He'd met the Iowa native last year, when she was dating his college buddy Tavares Butler. He'd been impressed with how intelligent she was, how lively and vivacious.

The actress was a down-home girl with a big personality, and he'd liked her instantly. When Tavares relocated to Australia last summer for work, he'd asked Dante to look out for her, and he'd readily agreed. Three months later, they'd called it quits, but he suspected Jordana was still in love with her ex. She didn't date, shot down everyone who asked her out and wouldn't set foot inside the club. They were friends, but that didn't stop Dante from admiring her from afar.

The jet stopped abruptly.

Dante stared out the window, but he didn't see what the holdup was. Thirsty, he picked up his glass and sipped some water. He needed something stronger. The bar was stocked with everything from Cristal to vodka, but he chose to grab a wine cooler. Designed with scrumptious Italian leather, designer fixtures and state-of-the art electronics, the jet had all the comforts of home, and everything Dante needed was at his fingertips.

Yawning, he rubbed the sleep from his eyes. His week-long business trip to Hong Kong had been taxing, filled with so many late nights and early mornings he felt both physically and mentally drained, though his time abroad had been productive, and he was excited about his latest business venture. The Brokerage Group wanted to build several commercial properties in Asia, and if everything went according to plan, the deal would go off without a hitch and he'd be lauded as a hero.

Ready to leave, Dante slipped on his aviator sunglasses. He'd been up since 5:00 a.m. and was looking forward to going home, putting up his feet and enjoying a cold beer. Or two. He deserved it. He worked fourteen-hour days, six days a week, and if not for the occasional brew—and Matteo—he'd probably be burned out.

Thoughts of his mischievous four-year-old son flooded Dante's mind. His smile couldn't be any wider, any brighter.

Matteo was his heart, his pride and joy, and his happiest moments were spent chasing him around the house, acting like a goofball to earn a laugh.

The intercom came on.

"I apologize for the delay, Mr. Morretti, but the Boeing 747 in front of us seems to be having mechanical issues and is stuck on the tarmac," the first officer explained. "We'll get you to the terminal as soon as we can. Thank you for your patience and understanding."

Dante returned to his seat, took his iPad out of his briefcase and turned it on. *Might as well get some work done while I wait*, he decided, typing in his password. The satellite phone sitting on the side table rang, and Dante answered it. Only a handful of people had the number, so he knew the call was important. The moment he heard the voice on the line, his heart stopped. It was his son's preschool teacher, Ms. Papadopoulos. She sounded troubled, flustered. What was wrong? Did something happen at Beverly Hills Preschool Academy? Panic ballooned inside his chest. Was Matteo hurt? Had he fallen off the jungle gym again?

"Is everything okay?" he asked, despite the knot stuck in his throat.

"Have you heard from your ex-wife?"

Dante frowned, gripping the receiver. "No, I haven't. Why? Is there a problem?"

"She's thirty minutes late to pick up Matteo, and she isn't answering her cell phone."

Thirty minutes! *Damn.* How could Lourdes forget to pick up his son? His ex-wife was punctually challenged, but whenever he had spoken to her about being on time she'd shrugged off his concerns. Lourdes had no reason to be late. She didn't work, hadn't held a nine-to-five in years, and even though she had joked being beautiful *was* a full-time job, it wasn't.

Hanging his head, he raked a hand through his thick black hair. Because of his furious work schedule, he'd agreed to let Lourdes have custody of Matteo, but he wondered for the umpteenth time if he'd made a grave mistake. His ex-wife was petty, thought the world revolved around her and used their son as a pawn. Dante wished Lourdes was a better mother—

Who are you to judge? his conscience interrupted. *You see Matteo only once a week.*

Dante felt helpless, as if his hands were tied. He wished there was something he could do, but he knew badmouthing his ex-wife to Ms. Papadopoulos was not the answer. He had always made a concerted effort to publicly support Lourdes, even when she was dead wrong, and he searched his mind for the right words to say. "I'm really sorry about this—"

"This behavior is unacceptable *and* hurtful to your son, as well. Every day, Matteo is the last child to get picked up from school, and it breaks my heart to see him cry."

"Ms. Papadopoulos, this won't happen again. You have my word."

"I hope so, Mr. Morretti, because the next time your ex-wife is late to pick up Matteo, I'm contacting the Department of Children and Family Services."

His spirits sank even lower.

"As an educator, I'm legally and morally obligated to report all forms of abuse and neglect to DCFS. I won't shirk my responsibilities."

Stunned, Dante couldn't speak. *Abuse? Neglect?* The words rattled around his head, blaring like a police siren. His temperature rose and sweat drenched his blue polo shirt. He felt inept, as if he'd failed as a parent, and his heart throbbed in pain.

Peering out the window, Dante noticed the plane was still hundreds of yards from the terminal, and he willed it to move faster. *Hurry up, dammit! I have to pick up my son!* Dante opened his mouth to speak, to plead with Ms. Papadopoulos for understanding, but she interrupted him.

"The principal wants to speak to you and your wife about this matter, as well."

"Ms. Papadopoulos, I'm on my way."

"We'll be waiting in the office. Please hurry. Matteo is very upset."

Click.

Dropping the phone in the cradle, Dante checked the time on his gold wristwatch. Four fifteen. It was rush hour, bumper-to-bumper traffic on the I-10. It would probably take an hour—or longer—to reach Matteo's preschool. *Where is Lourdes? How could she do this? I love Matteo more than anything. Doesn't she?*

Dante dialed Lourdes's cell number. He drummed his fingers on the table. Her voice mail came on, but her mailbox was full so he couldn't leave a message. Dante struck the armrest with his fist. Anger burned inside him, surging through his veins. It took everything in him not to punch the wall, every ounce of his self-control.

Expelling a deep breath, Dante considered his next move. He had to find someone to pick up Matteo before Ms. Papadopoulos made good on her threat and called the Department of Child and Family Services. Women's names and faces flashed in his mind, but since he'd never introduced any of his past lovers to his son, he didn't feel comfortable asking any of them to help out. Dante considered calling his brother, but he knew it was a waste of time. Markos was either in court, or on the golf course wooing potential clients. A divorce attorney to the stars, who was also a partner at a prestigious law firm, Markos was the most sought-after and esteemed lawyer in the city. He was dating three very different women—a surgeon, an engineer and a drama teacher—and often joked there was more than enough of him to go around.

"Jordana!" The name burst out of his mouth and ricocheted around the cabin. A week ago, she'd left abruptly for her hometown, and after numerous text messages he had learned her mom was sick. To cheer up Ms. Sharpe, he'd sent her a lavish flower bouquet and a gift basket. He'd never met Jordana's mother, but he hoped to one day, and planned to tell her she'd raised one hell of a woman. Was she back in town, or still taking care of her mom?

There was only one way to find out.

Dante punched in her cell number. Images of her scrolled through his mind, warming his heart. Jordana, with her bright smile and fun-loving personality, reminded him of his kid sister, Francesca. "Hello?"

Happy to hear her voice, he sighed in relief. "I need a favor."

"Hi, Dante! I'm fine. Thanks for asking. How are you?"

"I'm sorry. I didn't mean to be rude," he said, feeling contrite.

Jordana laughed. "Relax, buddy. I'm just kidding."

"How was your trip?" Dante asked. He didn't have time to shoot the breeze, but he was curious to know how her mother was doing. Based on past conversations they'd had, he knew Jordana adored her mom, and he hoped Ms. Sharpe was doing better.

"Good, but it's great to be back in LA. There's no place like home."

"You grew up in Des Moines, remember?"

Jordana groaned. "Ugh, don't remind me."

"How's your mom feeling? All better and on the mend?"

Silence infected the line. Several seconds passed before Jordana spoke.

"She's coming along," she said quietly, her tone losing

its warmth. "Thanks for sending her flowers. I don't think I've ever seen Helene so excited."

"It was my pleasure. I'm glad she liked them."

"You said you needed a favor. What is it?"

"Matteo's school just called," he explained, glancing out the window. He couldn't see anything, but Dante felt the plane moving and knew that was a good sign. "Lourdes was supposed to pick him up at three twenty-five, but she's missing in action, and I'm stuck at LAX."

"Oh, no, that's terrible. I hope she's okay—"

"Screw her," he snapped. "Lourdes doesn't deserve your pity. She's probably at home screwing the gardener in the house *I* paid millions for, and forgot all about my son."

"Dante, Matteo's her son, too, and I find it hard to believe she'd deliberately hurt him. I know you guys have had your problems in the past, but give Lourdes the benefit of the doubt..."

A bitter taste filled his mouth. Dante was pissed. Mad at himself for marrying Lourdes Faison four years ago. If he could turn back the hands of time, he never would've hooked up with the buxom hairstylist on New Year's Eve. They'd met at an upscale martini bar and had spent a wild, drunken night at his swank bachelor pad. Two months later, Dante learned he was going to be a father. It took weeks for him to come to terms with the news, then he'd done what any stand-up guy would do—he'd popped the question.

Dante scowled. He didn't have a choice; her father had threatened to kick his ass if he didn't. His heart wasn't in it, but since it was the right thing to do, he'd played the role of the devoted fiancé. But just days after their lavish, three-hundred-guest wedding in Palm Springs, Dante had realized he'd made a huge mistake. Lourdes complained incessantly, spent money recklessly and treated his staff like crap. In spite of her diva behavior, he remained committed to their relationship. Coming home from work and seeing his infant son was the highlight of his day. It was what gave him the strength to endure a loveless marriage.

His thoughts wandered, returning to the worst day of his life. One week after their two-year anniversary, Lourdes left their estate with Matteo and filed for divorce. Dante never saw it coming, was blindsided by her deception and betrayal. She went on to publicly humiliate him, telling sensational stories to the newspapers that tarnished his reputation. He'd never forgive her for vilifying him in the press.

"Do you want me to pick up Matteo? I can go get him right now."

Relief flooded Dante's body. He could breathe again. "I'll call Matteo's school and let them know you're coming. Thanks, Jordana. You're the best!"

"I know, and you can tell me how *fabulous* I am the next time we have lunch at Spago. I'm an aspiring actress who can't afford to eat at fancy restaurants, so it's your treat!"

"I'll take you anywhere you want—"

Hearing the intercom, he broke off speaking and listened intently.

The first officer thanked him for his patience, and Dante jumped to his feet. Putting on his sunglasses, he grabbed his suitcase and marched through the cabin. "I'm leaving LAX now," he said, jogging down the aisle. "I'll be there as fast as I can."

"Don't rush. I'm going to take Matteo to the park to feed the pigeons."

"Thanks again, Jordana."

"No worries, friend. I'll see you soon."

Anxious to see his son—and to give his good-for-nothing ex-wife a piece of his mind—Dante jogged down the steps, ducked into the white Lincoln Navigator waiting on the tarmac and told the middle-aged driver to step on it.

Chapter 2

Dante arrived at the Pacific Palisades apartment complex at six o'clock, annoyed he'd spent the past two hours stuck in traffic. Worse, he still hadn't heard from Lourdes. As the car drove to the entrance of the building, he spotted three men dressed in basketball jerseys and jeans idling near the glass doors. They were smoking, guffawing so loud Dante could hear them through the car windows. He wondered for the umpteenth time why Jordana wouldn't move to a better area. One with less crime and graffiti and fewer nefarious characters.

La Brea, a diverse, multicultural neighborhood nestled between downtown and Hollywood, was known for its unique architecture, eclectic boutiques and restaurants, and vibrant nightlife. Dante had rental properties all across the city, in posh, affluent neighborhoods such as Bel Air and South Valley, but whenever he encouraged Jordana to move, she'd say, "I can't leave La Brea. I love it here! These are my people!" Dante didn't know what that meant, found it odd that she enjoyed the company of hoods and scoundrels, but he kept his thoughts to himself. Although he owned several office buildings in the area, he rarely visited La Brea, and couldn't remember the last time he'd been to Jordana's apartment.

Stepping out of the car, he nodded at the men in greeting. They gave him the once-over and grunted in response. Dante strode through the front doors and into the sunny foyer.

Taking off his sunglasses, he wrinkled his nose. The air held the scent of onions, the reception area looked in need of an extreme makeover, and tenants were standing around waiting for the elevator, complaining about management, the recent string of apartment break-ins and last month's exorbitant rent increase.

Seconds passed, then minutes, but there was no sign of the elevator.

Growing impatient, Dante stalked through the lobby and ducked into the stairwell. Hearing his iPhone ring, he stopped in his tracks and retrieved it from his pocket. He read the name on the screen, and his eyes thinned and his face hardened like stone. Now *she wants to call back. Almost two hours later? Is Lourdes out of her damn mind?*

Fuming, he put his cell to his ear and gave voice to his anger. "Where the hell have you been?" he demanded, unable to govern his temper. "Ms. Papadopoulos called me in a panic because you forgot to pick up Matteo. What's the matter with you? Are you trying to get us in trouble with Child and Family Services?"

Lourdes yawned, then spoke in a drowsy voice. "I'm sorry. I dozed off while watching TV and I just woke up a few minutes ago."

"Where's Nayoko?"

"I had to fire her. She was stealing from me."

"Sure she was," Dante grumbled, shaking his head in

disbelief. This wasn't the first time Lourdes had fired a nanny, and it probably wouldn't be the last. His ex-wife loved playing the victim and would do anything for attention, even make up stories about her staff.

"It's the truth. Why would I lie?"

Because you're a habitual liar, he thought but didn't say. "I called you more than a dozen times. You didn't hear your cell phone ringing off the hook?"

"It hasn't been working properly."

Dante didn't believe her. He was tired of her lies and half-truths. He couldn't stomach more of her bullshit today. "Did you go to the bar at lunch? Is that why you forgot to pick up Matteo? Because you're drunk?"

The silence was deafening, and it confirmed his worst fears. Fighting with Lourdes wasn't the answer; it wouldn't solve anything. But he had to get through to her. "Tell me the truth."

"I just did."

Dante wanted answers, and he wasn't letting Lourdes off the hook until she came clean. Since the divorce, he'd tried to keep the peace, to be the bigger person, but not this time. He had to speak his mind. "You need to get yourself together. Matteo should be your number one priority, not drinking or your stupid friends."

"I said I'm sorry."

"Sorry isn't good enough."

"We can't all be perfect like you," she shot back, her tone heavy with sarcasm. "So quit giving me a hard time for being human, and let me talk to my son—"

"This isn't about being perfect. This is about being a good parent."

"I messed up. There, I said it. Is that what you want to hear? Happy now?"

Dante cocked an eyebrow. *Did I hear her right?* Lourdes

never, *ever* owned up to her mistakes, even when she was wrong. His ears had to be playing tricks on him.

"None of this would've happened if you'd paid for me to have a chauffeured car."

Cha-ching! Shaking his head, he stared down at his cell phone with disgust. It didn't matter what the issue was, Lourdes always found a way to make it about money. Up to her neck in debt, she couldn't afford to maintain her extravagant lifestyle, and she expected him to continue supporting her. Hell, no. Lourdes was spoiled, and he refused to indulge her every whim. Matteo didn't need a chauffeured car, or three live-in nannies, or any of the other expensive crap she wanted money for. Her monthly alimony check was more than the average person earned in a year, and he wasn't giving her another dime. "If you want a chauffeured car, then pay for it yourself," he snapped. "Pick up Matteo on time—"

"Don't tell me what to do. You're not the boss of me, and I don't have to listen to you."

"This isn't about me. This is about doing what's best for our son."

"You're not my husband anymore, remember? I dumped you for a real man..."

The insult hit him like a fist to the gut. There were hard feelings on both sides, years of pent-up anger and frustration, but Dante held his tongue. He knew the truth and that was all that mattered. During their marriage, he'd honored his vows, and respected her as his spouse. Unfortunately, Lourdes couldn't say the same.

"What time are you bringing Matteo home?"

"Why? It's not like you care about him..." Realizing his mistake, he winced and slammed his mouth shut. It was too late; the damage had been done. The line went dead, and guilt troubled his conscience.

Ending the call, Dante chastised himself for losing his

cool. Lourdes brought out the worst in him, always had, but he had no right to disrespect her. He'd apologize later, when he dropped Matteo off, and then he'd have an honest talk with her about his concerns. Lourdes had to do better, had to start putting their son first or… Dante trailed off, couldn't finish his sentence.

Or what? questioned his inner voice. *What are you going to do? Quit your high-paying, jet-setting job and become a stay-at-home dad?*

The thought was outrageous, laughable even, but Dante didn't chuckle. There was nothing funny about his predicament. He was worried about his son's well-being and needed sound advice. But not from Emilio and Immanuel. His brothers were living the American dream, so happy in love they talked about their significant others nonstop. Dante didn't want to hear about how wonderful their partners were. Not when Lourdes was making his life a living hell. He had to talk to Markos, and the sooner the better.

On the fourth floor, Dante stopped in front of apartment 4B and rang the buzzer.

The door swung open and Matteo jumped into his arms. "Daddy!"

Chuckling, Dante held him tight and spun him around the hallway.

"Faster, Daddy! Faster!"

Dante obliged, and his son shrieked with laughter. The sound warmed his heart, made him feel like the world's best dad. Matteo was his number one concern, the only person in his life who truly mattered, and he'd do anything to make him happy. He looked adorable in his navy blue uniform, like the spitting image of his grandfather, but with dark, curly hair.

"Daddy, where's Mommy? She forgot to pick me up from school today."

"Mommy's at home, li'l man. You'll see her later."

"Great timing. Dinner's almost ready."

Dante put Matteo down and faced Jordana. Her smile blinded him with its light. His pulse sped up. In a city overrun with females addicted to plastic surgery, it was refreshing to see a natural woman. Her beauty boggled his mind, leaving him tongue-tied and weak in the knees. Even in a tie-dye shirt and denim shorts, Jordana was stunning. She looked pretty and youthful in her outfit, and smelled like heaven. She had eyes a man could get lost in, tawny skin dotted with freckles and a shapely physique. Dante loved how lush and thick her hair was, and his hands itched to play in her chocolate-brown curls. She'd been blessed with model features and a banging body, but she wasn't a snob. Everywhere Jordana went she made friends and men tripped over themselves to meet her. Even A-list celebrities.

"I'm starving," Dante said, patting his empty stomach. "What's on the menu?"

"Squash soup, kale-almond salad and chickpea burgers."

He wrinkled his nose. "I just lost my appetite."

"Oh, stop. Vegan food is to die for."

"Yeah, if you're stranded on a deserted island."

"You're not happy unless you're eating a hundred-dollar steak. But don't come crying to me the next time we go to a fancy five-star Beverly Hills restaurant and you get chest pains."

"I didn't get chest pains because of the food." Dante winked, flashing her a mischievous grin to make her laugh. "It was that sexy little hostess in the see-through dress. What a hottie!"

Jordana stuck out her tongue, and Dante chuckled. His gaze zeroed in on her mouth, lingering there for a beat. *Those are some lips*, he thought, wishing they were pressed against his. He liked how plump they were, how moist and juicy they looked.

Catching himself, he tore his eyes away from her face. They were friends and nothing more, and that would never change. Jordana was like a sister to him—

Bullshit! argued his inner voice. *Sister, my ass! You want her bad, and the only reason you haven't made a play for her is because she's still in love with her ex.*

"Dad, can we stay for dinner? Please?" Matteo begged. "I just *love* cheeseburgers."

"That depends. Were you a good boy for Jordana?"

"No," she said sadly, shaking her head. "He was horrible."

"He was?"

"Yup. The worst."

Dante spoke in a stern voice. "You have some explaining to do, young man."

Eyes wide with alarm, Matteo glanced frantically from his dad to Jordana. "I didn't mean to spill grape juice on the carpet," he said, shuffling his feet. "It was an accident, but I cleaned it up right away. Tell him, Jordana. Tell my dad I was a good boy."

"You weren't good," she said, ruffling his curly hair. "You were *great*."

Matteo cheered. "Dad, did you bring me something back from King Kong?"

"I went to Hong Kong," Dante said with a laugh. "King Kong is a character in a movie."

"Oops!" Giggling, he spun around and took off running back inside the apartment.

Jordana waved him inside and closed the door. "Have you heard from Lourdes?" she whispered, her features touched with concern. "Is she okay?"

"Apparently she fell asleep and just woke up a few minutes ago."

"You don't believe her?"

"No, she's a compulsive liar who can't be trusted."

"Don't be so hard on her. Everyone has a bad day."

Following her down the hallway, he sniffed the air. A spicy aroma tickled his nose, and his stomach grumbled. Dante hated vegan food, but the apartment smelled so good his mouth watered with hungry anticipation.

"How's the sweatshop?" he asked jokingly. After six years of being a nanny, Jordana had quit to pursue a career in acting. But after months of pounding the pavement with no luck, she'd accepted a job at a telemarketing agency. Dante loved independent women, but it bothered him that she didn't tell him about her financial troubles. Typical Jordana. She'd rather suffer in silence than accept help. Her I'm-every-woman attitude drove him crazy. He loved showering his family and friends with gifts, and he wanted to spoil Jordana, too, but she wouldn't let him. "Are you still thinking about quitting?"

"Every second of every day," she quipped, entering the kitchen. Sliding on her cooking mitts, she bent over, opened the oven and took out the casserole dish. "It's paying the bills, so I'm trying not to complain."

"Come work for me." It was a struggle to be a gentleman, but Dante kept his eyes on the wall clock and off her delicious backside. He'd never seen a pair of jean shorts look better, and he liked how they elongated her long brown legs. "I could use another executive assistant, and I think you'd be an asset to The Brokerage Group."

"I'd never fit in at your company."

"Why not? You're smart, and beautiful, and—"

"Curvy," she added, with a flick of her head. "You only hire tall, thin, surgically enhanced blondes, and that's not me. Besides, my dream is to be an actress, not an executive assistant. I suck at answering phones, and I don't know how to make coffee."

"I don't drink coffee. I drink tea."

"Tea?" Jordana wore a funny face. "And you say you're *not* a metrosexual? Right!"

Chuckling, he leaned against the wall and crossed his arms. Watching Jordana move around the kitchen made Dante think of all the times he'd returned home from work and found Lourdes and Matteo baking cookies.

Memories of happier days flashed in his mind. Playing soccer in the backyard, swimming, reading him bedtime stories. Dante talked big, pretended he didn't need anyone, but he missed having his family around. That's why he worked nonstop and traveled as much as he did. Work helped him forget his pain, his loneliness. Feeling a pang of sadness, he shook off his thoughts and wiped at his eyes with his fingertips.

"Here," Jordana said, raising a silver serving spoon in the air. "Try this. It's amazing."

The soup was thick, seasoned with Italian herbs and filled with vegetables. It smelled good, like his grandmother's tortellini stew. Since Dante was starving, he opened his mouth wide. He puckered his lips and scrunched up his nose. Swallowing hard, he forced the liquid down his throat, then rubbed a hand across his chest to alleviate the burning sensation.

"What do you think?"

"I think you should let me take you out for dinner."

Her face fell. "You don't like it?"

No, but I like you. You're sweet and considerate, and you're great with my son.

"Oh, well, it's your loss, because my squash soup is not only healthy but delicious."

"I'd rather have a hundred-dollar steak."

Jordana pointed at the hallway. "Get out, before I throw you out!"

Dante chuckled. He wanted to talk to Jordana about his argument with Lourdes, but the kitchen was small and cramped, and he didn't want to crowd her. Matteo was sitting at the kitchen table, coloring in his Batman-themed sketch pad. Seeing his son happy made Dante smile. "Fine," he said. "I'm going to go watch the Royals game."

"Knock yourself out."

Exiting the kitchen, he admired the pictures hanging on the walls. The two-bedroom apartment was filled with knickknacks and secondhand furniture. But since his mother had taught him not to look down on people, he took a seat on the battered beige couch and swiped the remote control off the coffee table. Pointing it at the flat-screen TV, he searched for the baseball game on one of the local stations. His favorite sport was boxing, but since his cousin Demetri Morretti was the biggest baseball star on the planet, and also one of his wealthiest clients, Dante made a point to watch his games.

A sly grin warmed his mouth. They used to party like rock stars, but now that his cousin was happily married to his newscaster wife, Dante rarely saw him. He was looking forward to seeing his brothers and cousins at the end of July at the RaShawn Bishop Celebrity Golf tournament in Tampa. He was planning an impromptu bachelor party for Immanuel as well, and he couldn't wait to see the look on his brother's face when the exotic dancers he'd secretly booked stormed his hotel suite. Immanuel was tying the knot at the end of the year, and Dante wanted him to live it up one last time before his walk down the aisle.

"I swear, if I wasn't madly in love with my boyfriend, I'd dump him and marry you!"

Dante cranked his head to the right, and spotted Jordana's roommate standing in the hallway. He nodded his head in greeting. Waverly Burke was a heavy-set brunette in her midtwenties who looked decades older. She liked to flirt, and seemed to get a kick out of shocking him. .

"I bought *LA Business* magazine yesterday and almost

passed out when I saw the pictures of your new Bel Air estate. I knew you were rich, but I had no idea you were *that* rich." Her eyes were wide with wonder, and she spoke in a reverent tone. "I still don't understand what you do, though. Is a real estate developer like an architect?"

"No. My job is to purchase existing and undeveloped real estate properties and sell or lease the building for a profit."

"Sounds risky. What if something goes wrong, or the property doesn't sell?"

"That's all part of the job. But with great risk comes great reward," Dante said, repeating his personal mantra. "I work my ass off to ensure that doesn't happen, and my persistence and determination has served me well in this cutthroat business."

"I'd say. You're rich and famous and your mansion is bigger than the White House!"

Jordana poked her head into the room. "Money isn't everything, Waverly. Celebrities have fears and insecurities just like the rest of us, if not more."

That's right, Jordana. Tell her! The more money I make, the more problems I have.

"As if. Deciding what to wear to a movie premiere is hardly a serious dilemma."

"I was a nanny for several high-profile couples, and trust me, being an A-lister is not as glamorous as it seems. They have zero privacy, and everything they say and do is scrutinized."

Waverly snorted. "Wah, wah, wah. Cry me a river. That's what they signed up for!"

"You're not being fair."

"Spare me. Celebrities have the best of everything, but they're always bitching and complaining about how hard life is. Ugh. Rich people make me sick." Her cheeks turned beet red, and a sheepish expression appeared on her face. "Present company excluded of course."

Jordana caught Dante's eye and mouthed, "Be nice. She's my best friend."

Nodding, he smiled to assure her everything was okay. And it was. Dante was used to women talking crazy and asking him personal questions, especially about Emilio—one of the best race-car drivers of all time—so he didn't take offense to her roommate's comments. Waverly was hilarious, outspoken and brash, and Dante wanted to get to know her better.

Yeah, agreed his inner voice. *So she can help you win over Jordana!*

"Is it true you have five brothers?" Waverly asked.

"Yes, and three are single."

Waverly licked her lips. "Do tell."

"Romeo is an investment banker based in Milan, Enrique is an entrepreneur with a slew of successful exotic-car dealerships in Europe and Markos is a celebrity divorce lawyer here in LA."

"I'll take the divorce attorney," she said quickly, with a girlish laugh. "Mrs. Waverly Morretti sounds classy and sophisticated, don't you think?"

"One tall, dark and handsome attorney coming right up!"

The women cracked up, and the sound made his chest puff up with pride. Dante loved making Jordana laugh, and would poke fun at himself just to see her smile. Always positive and upbeat, she was a light who glowed from within, and he enjoyed spending time with her—even though her heart belonged to another man.

"Dinner's served," Jordana announced, gesturing to the table. "Let's eat. I'm famished."

"You guys go ahead." Dante found the Chicago Royals game on TV, used the remote control to increase the volume, and scanned the dugout for his cousin. "I'm not hungry."

Her eyes narrowed, darkened. "You're still expected to sit at the table."

By whom? he thought, confused by her words. "I'm watching the game."

Planting her hands on her hips, she flashed him an are-you-out-of-your-mind expression and Dante knew he was in trouble. He'd seen her angry only once—when he'd "accidentally" deposited money into her bank account—and he shuddered at the memory of their explosive argument on Christmas Eve. She'd returned the money, after cursing him out in English *and* Spanish. To this day he still didn't understand why she'd gone ballistic on him.

"My house, my rules," she quipped, pointing at an empty chair. "Now, *sit*."

Her bossy, take-charge attitude made his erection rise and his mouth wet. Jordana was a freethinker who wasn't afraid to speak her mind, and Dante enjoyed her fiery, spirited personality. They couldn't be more different, and had nothing in common. Logical and decisive, Dante knew what he wanted out of life, where he was going and how to get there. Jordana, on the other hand, was still finding herself. She was as carefree as a butterfly in the wind.

"You're too pretty to be so mean," he joked, hoping to make her laugh. "Be nice, Jordana, or I'll call your mom and tell her you're bullying me!"

Jordana's scowl deepened, wrinkling her smooth skin, but Waverly cracked up.

"Good one," she said. "And if you need her mom's number just let me know."

Hearing his cell phone beep, he took it out of his pocket. The text was from Lourdes, and she wasn't happy. Reading her message annoyed him. For the second time that evening Dante wondered what he'd ever seen in the celebrity hairstylist.

Where are you? Bring Matteo home now or else...

A scowl curled his lips. Lourdes had some nerve telling him what to do. But since he wanted to keep the peace, he stood, took his car keys out of his back pocket and switched off the television. "I better take Matteo home. It's a school night."

"I understand." Jordana nodded, dropping her hands at her sides. "Maybe next time."

"But I don't want to go. I want to stay for dessert."

Crouching beside Matteo's chair, she smiled and touched his cheek. "You can take some brownies with you. How does that sound?"

"Great!" Beaming, Matteo gathered his things, throwing them inside his backpack.

"Thanks again, Jordana. I owe you one."

"No problem. That's what friends are for."

Minutes later, Dante left the apartment with Matteo in tow, carrying a container filled with vegan brownies. As they boarded the elevator, Dante noticed Jordana waving at them, and he smiled in return. He loved her energy, how bubbly and effervescent she was, and as the elevator doors slid closed a curious thought—one he'd had many times in recent months—popped into his mind. *Why couldn't I have married someone like Jordana? Someone warm and loving and caring who puts others' needs above her own?*

It's not too late, said his inner voice, drowning out the doubts playing in his mind. *Make your move and let the chips fall where they may.*

Dante rejected the thought, refusing to consider it. Jordana was smart, with a great head on her shoulders, but they could never be a couple. There were just some things a man didn't do, especially a man of his stature, and hooking up with a friend's ex was one of them. He desired her, sure, but some rules weren't meant to be broken.

Chapter 3

Jordana was miserable, more depressed than a high school senior without a prom date, and her telemarketing job was the reason why. Only three hours into her shift, and she wanted to go home and crawl into bed. Massaging her temples, she kicked off her gold ballet flats, and took a moment to gather herself. Ringing telephones, animated chatter and country music filled the air. The incessant noise inside LA Marketing Enterprises made it hard for her to think.

Her thoughts wandered, returning to the conversation she'd had with the loud, hostile Texan minutes earlier. Making fundraising calls on behalf of charitable organizations was an honorable endeavor, something to be proud of, but Jordana was tired of being a human punching bag. People insulted her on a daily basis, calling her horrible, vulgar names. But she couldn't defend herself. She'd worked numerous jobs since moving to LA, everything from waitressing to babysitting and tutoring, but nothing was more intolerable than being a telemarketer.

What have I done? What was I thinking? Why did I leave my cushy job with the Robinson family? The weight of her despair was crushing, but there was nothing Jordana could do about it. *Not unless I want to be homeless*, she thought glumly, feeling her shoulders sag. A year ago, she was a live-in nanny, taking care of an autistic child in Bel Air, and although she loved the two-year-old boy as if he were her own, she hated the long hours. She couldn't attend casting calls, lost touch with her girlfriends and rarely had days off. For that reason, she'd resigned, moved in with her best friend, Waverly Burke, and decided to pursue her dreams wholeheartedly. Her agent, Fallon O'Neal, was sweet, but tough when she had to be. Jordana knew the former child star had her best interests in heart.

Jordana straightened in her chair, and adjusted her headset. Slapping a smile on her face, she greeted the caller. "Hello, Mr. Okafor," she said, with fake enthusiasm. "How are you doing this morning?"

"Who's this?" croaked a male voice, with a heavy Nigerian accent. "What do you want?"

"I'm glad you asked. My name is Jordana Sharpe, and I'm calling on behalf of—"

"Damn telemarketers," he grumbled, interrupting her. "Why are you harassing me? Don't you have better things to do than ruin my day off?"

Jordana pressed her lips together to trap a scream inside. No matter what he said, she'd remain on the line. She had no choice. If she hung up, she'd be sent home without pay, and Jordana needed her paycheck.

"I understand that you are busy, so I will keep this brief."

"Don't call here again, stupid."

Click.

Swiping off her headset, she dropped it on the desk, and slumped in her chair. Jordana released a deep breath, reminding herself not to take the caller's comments personally. Her job was mentally and emotionally draining, and Jordana didn't know how much more she could take. She had to put up with being verbally abused—all day, every day—and no one cared. Last month, she'd met with her supervisor, Mr. Lundqvist, but instead of being sympathetic, he'd told her to "suck it up and quit complaining." Each week things got worse. Jordana wanted out.

But how? If I quit, I won't be able to pay my rent, or enroll in acting classes. Staring up at the ceiling, with tears in her eyes, Jordana wondered if and when she'd ever get her "big break." She'd been in LA for six years, and had nothing to show for it except debt, heartache and stress. Maybe her father, Fernán, was right; maybe she was fooling herself. Maybe it was time to pack it up and head home. *He had said I'd never make it in this town, and I'm starting to believe him.*

Tears pricked her eyes, and emotion clogged her throat, making it hard to swallow. The thought of leaving Los Angeles and returning to Des Moines saddened her. Everything she'd ever wanted was in LA, and she wasn't ready—or willing—to concede defeat. At least not yet. Jordana snapped out of it, willing herself to be strong. She had an audition tomorrow and a meeting with her agent on Monday. If everything went according to plan she'd be one step closer to fulfilling her dream. She wasn't giving up now, or ever. It didn't matter what her dad or anyone else said. She *would* make it.

A tear spilled down her cheek, and Jordana slapped it away. Needing a moment to compose herself, she put on her shoes, and stood. At times like this, when she was feeling emotional and upset, a change of scenery helped improve her mood. A five-minute break was definitely in order.

"Where do you think *you're* going?"

Glancing over her shoulder, she noticed her supervisor standing in the hallway, and strangled a groan. Mr. Lundqvist was a control freak, with bad breath, and his toothy grin made her skin crawl. "I'm going to the ladies' room."

"Again?" He raised a thick, bushy eyebrow. "You just went."

No, I didn't. Even if I did, what's it to you? He was in her cubicle, questioning her no less, and had the nerve to look pissed, as if she was giving *him* the third degree for leaving his desk. Making a conscious decision not to raise her voice, she forced an easy-breezy smile, and spoke in a soft tone. "That's not true," she said calmly, resisting the urge to kick him in the shin. "I haven't left my desk since I arrived this morning."

"Fine." Scowling, his face twisted in anger, he tapped the front of his watch with an index finger. "Hurry up. You have two minutes, not a second more."

Glaring at him, Jordana wondered how many times he'd been dropped on his head as a child. She wanted to tell Mr. Lundqvist to jump off the nearest bridge, but remembered her rent was due at the end of the mouth, and bit the inside of her cheek.

"Get going, Sharpe. I'm timing you."

Jordana grabbed her tote bag and fled her cubicle. Walking through the office, she noticed how bleak the mood was and stared out the window. Thick clouds covered the sky, and smog cast a dark haze over the city. The dreary weather mirrored her disposition, but Jordana was determined not to wallow in self-pity. She had a lot to be thankful for. She had great friends, auditions coming up, and the best news of all, her mom was healthy again. Painful memories surfaced, but she quickly shook them off, making up her mind to focus on the future, not the past.

In the washroom, Jordana touched up her makeup and assessed her look. Peering into the mirror, she adjusted her leather beaded headband. Her tunic-style dress skimmed her hips, and her fringed sandals drew attention to her legs. Thanks to her Cuban father and Haitian mother, she had wild, unruly curls, a complexion smoother than honey and more curves than a winding road. Dante told her she had an exotic, one-of-a-kind look, but in a city overrun with beautiful women, Jordana didn't know if he was telling the truth or just being nice.

Images of him filled her mind and a smile overwhelmed her mouth. Dante was one of her best friends, someone she could count on. Jordana felt fortunate to have him in her life. On the surface, they seemed to have nothing in common. She was a small-town girl from a broken home living paycheck to paycheck, and he was a real estate mogul who made millions in his sleep. Surprisingly, their differences drew them together, not apart. Once a week they met at his favorite pub, and over appetizers, they'd have long, intense discussions.

Curious how Dante was doing—and her favorite four-year-old, Matteo—Jordana took her cell phone out of her bag and punched in her password. To her surprise, she had a new text message from Dante, and although it was only two sentences, it made her feel incredibly special. No surprise. The high-powered businessman was in a league of his own, and his thoughtfulness never ceased to amaze her. He wanted to take her to lunch at the best Italian restaurant in the city, and the thought of seeing him again excited her. Funny, considering the first time they met she thought he was an arrogant prick. Over time, she'd realized there was more to Dante than what met the eye, and they'd become fast friends.

Before she could respond to his message, her cell phone rang, and her mom's picture popped up on the screen.

Dread churned inside the pit of her stomach. Her mom didn't call often, only when there was a problem at home, and Jordana feared the worst. What was it this time? Was her mom short on money again? Was she calling to beg her to come back home?

Conquering her nerves, she blew out a deep breath, and hit the FaceTime button. A gasp fell from her lips. Mascara stained her mom's cheeks, and her hair was disheveled, sticking up in every direction. As a child, she'd thought her mom was the most beautiful woman in the world, but life hadn't been kind to her, and the dark circles under her eyes made her look older than her fifty-eight years. "Mom, what's wrong?"

"I—I—I got another letter from Wells Fargo," she stammered.

Confused, she frowned and shook her head. "Another letter?" she repeated, trying to make sense of her mother's words. "When did you receive the first one?"

Helene sniffed, hanging her head.

"Talk to me, Mom. I want to know what's going on."

"I didn't want to bother you at work, but when I read the notice I got scared and I didn't know who else to call..." Trailing off, she wiped at her eyes. "I thought of giving your brothers a ring, but these days they never pick up when I call. It's like they're avoiding me."

"Mom, don't worry. You're not bothering me. I can talk." It was a lie, she couldn't, but Jordana didn't want to make her mom feel worse than she already did.

Glancing at her bracelet-style watch, she realized she'd been gone for six minutes, and hoped her supervisor wasn't actually timing her. Mr. Lundqvist took great pleasure in embarrassing people, especially the female staff. But at the moment, Jordana didn't care. Helene was upset, and she wasn't going to abandon her mom in her time of need.

"I'm going to lose my house…the house I raised you and your brothers in…"

Hearing a bang, Jordana cranked her head to the right. What was that?

"Jordana, are you in there? You've been gone seven minutes. If you don't come out *right* this instant I'm writing you up for insubordination!"

Startled, she stared at the bathroom door. Her supervisor was yelling her name like a deranged lunatic, but Jordana didn't move. Screw him. She'd explain the situation to him later, and if that didn't work, she'd take the matter to HR. She wasn't letting a psycho with a superiority complex bully her.

The banging stopped, and Jordana released the breath she was holding.

"Mom, I have to get back to work, but can you read me the letter before I go?"

Panic streaked across her face. Growing up in Haiti in a family of eight, her mother had never gone to elementary school. She didn't learn to read and write until she immigrated to America at nineteen. In spite of the setbacks she'd faced, Helene had tried her best to be a good mother. She didn't always get it right, and continued to struggle with her own inner demons, but Jordana adored her mom, loved her more than anything in the world.

Her dad was another story.

At the thought of him, her stomach churned. Fernán, was an athletic recruiter for a professional soccer team. The more money he'd made, the less time he'd spent with their family. He traveled the world, living it up like a frat boy with no responsibilities. Jordana resented him for leaving them behind. And for favoring her two older brothers, Carlito and Raymon. She'd never had a good relationship with her dad, not even when she was a kid, and these days they rarely spoke. They'd had a heated argument at Carlito's wedding, and a year later Jordana was still seething about the hurtful things he'd said about Helene. For that reason she'd never ask him for financial help. "Take your time, Mom. You can do it."

Jordana heard papers ruffle, watching as her mom wiped her tear-stained cheeks, and put on her eyeglasses. "Go ahead," she prompted, with a nod of encouragement. "I'm listening."

Helene straightened in her chair. Holding her head up high, she rested a hand on her chest and cleared her throat.

"Dear Ms. Sharpe. This letter is a formal notification that you are in default of your obligation to make payments on your home loan, account number 573189. This account holds a current sum of thirty-nine thousand dollars, payable on June 30…"

Her mom struggled to read some of the words, but it didn't matter. It was a foreclosure notice, the worst piece of mail a homeowner could ever receive, and the more Helene read, the sicker Jordana felt. Slumping against the tile wall, she touched a hand to her clammy face. Her mouth watered, craving a cold drink to quench her thirst. In the past, when she felt stressed, she'd hit the clubs with her girlfriends, dancing and drinking for hours.

God, I'd do anything for a— Jordana pressed her eyes shut, blocked the thought from entering her mind. *I've changed. I'm a different person now. And I won't live in the past.*

"This amount has been overdue for ninety days, and you have ignored multiple requests to make a payment," Helene continued. "Unless the current sum is paid by the listed due date, we have no choice but to begin the foreclosure process on your home…"

The air thinned, and the walls closed in, making it impossible for Jordana to breathe. Her head was spinning, throbbing in pain, and her throat was so dry it hurt to talk. "Ninety days? Mom, why haven't you been making your mortgage payments?"

"I didn't have the money. My hours were cut, and I don't have any savings."

Jordana nodded in understanding. Her mom earned peanuts as a housekeeper, and the families she worked for often canceled at the last minute. "I was just there. Why didn't you say anything? I could have gone with you to the bank and spoken to the loan officer."

Helene dropped her gaze to her lap. "I was embarrassed and ashamed."

Jordana's heart overflowed with sympathy. Her mom was a proud woman who'd rather go without than ask for help. Jordana understood. She was the same way. *What am I going to do?* Her salary was barely enough to support herself, let alone Helene. But she'd never forgive herself if she stood by and let the bank take her mother's home. She considered calling her dad, but he'd made it abundantly clear, on more than one occasion, that Helene wasn't his responsibility anymore. Her parents had never legally married, and after twelve years together her father had checked out of the relationship, leaving her mother to fend for herself. Her mom had been in financial troubles for as long as she could remember, but even during her worst moments, she'd never seen Helene lose her smile. Until today. She was shaking, sobbing uncontrollably, nothing like the strong, confident woman who'd raised her. "Mom, don't cry."

"I don't want to lose the house. It's all I have."

"You won't. We'll think of something."

Helene dabbed at her eyes with her fingertips. "We will?"

"Of course. We're in this together, right, Mom?"

A sad smile touched her lips. "But, the letter says—"

"I don't care what the letter says. I'll get the money."

"How?" Helene reached into her blouse, took out a Kleenex and blew her nose. "Your brothers will never help, and you earn minimum wage."

Mom, I know, don't remind me.

"I'll think of something. Just trust me, okay?"

"I don't know what I'd do without you," she said quietly. "You're such a good girl."

"Mom, I have to go. Are you going to your meeting tonight?"

The silence was deafening, lasting so long Jordana had to repeat the question.

"I don't feel like it. Not tonight. I want to stay home."

Jordana didn't push. Not this time. "Okay, Mom. I'll call you later."

"Have a good day, honey. I love you."

"I love you, too, Mom. Try not to worry."

Ending the call, she dropped her cell in her purse, and tiptoed toward the bathroom door. Opening it, she peered down the hall, in search of her crotchety supervisor. Finding the coast clear, she hustled down the corridor as fast as her ballet flats could take her.

Approaching her cubicle, she heard male voices, and frowned. Her supervisor was talking to someone, and the person sounded a lot like Dante. No way. It couldn't be. He was surely at his fancy downtown office, not at LA Marketing Enterprises shooting the breeze with her cranky boss.

Turning the corner, she felt her eyes widen and her legs wobble. Jordana stood there, with her mouth agape, unable to believe what she was seeing. *Is this for real? Is my supervisor actually laughing with Dante, or am I dreaming with my eyes open?*

"There you are!" her supervisor said brightly, his smile showcasing every crooked tooth. "I was just telling Mr.

Morretti what a valuable member you are of the LA Marketing team, and how much I enjoy working with you."

That confirmed it. She was dreaming. Had to be. There was no way in hell her supervisor was publicly praising her. Yelling and screaming, yes; compliments, no.

"Ms. Sharpe, are you okay?"

Dante moved in close, and rested his hand on her arm, giving it a light squeeze.

Goose bumps tickled her skin, and her temperature rose. He was a friend, but he was also a man—a very attractive man who reeked of masculinity—and his touch excited her. In his designer sunglasses and impeccable black suit, Dante was the picture of a young debonair professional at the top of his game. He was hot, no doubt about it, but his appeal didn't lie in his soulful eyes, and dreamy grin, but in his extraordinary generosity.

"You look upset. Is something the matter?"

Before Jordana could answer, her supervisor spoke up. "Of course not. She's excited about your business lunch, and anxious to tell you about our wonderful agency."

Jordana reclaimed her voice. "What business lunch?"

"Ms. Sharpe, I hope you haven't forgotten our plans."

What plans? We don't have any! she wanted to scream, giving him a bewildered, what-are-you-talking-about look. *And why are you calling me Ms. Sharpe? We're friends, not strangers. Heck, I've known you for almost two years!*

"No, no, of course not," Mr. Lundqvist said, adamantly shaking his head. He gave Jordana a shove, practically pushing her into Dante's arms. He spoke in a loud, booming voice, drawing the attention of everyone in the office. One by one, her colleagues poked their heads out of their cubicles. They all wore curious expressions on their faces, and the women were slobbering all over their fancy designer clothes.

That was no surprise. Dante attracted attention everywhere he went.

The real estate mogul had a reputation among women, and the house parties at his Beverly Hills mansion were legendary, but he was more than just a handsome face and hot body. He had a keen mind for business, was as gregarious as they came, and was a great listener. He was, without a doubt, the smartest person Jordana knew, and she valued his friendship. He was always teaching her new things—such as how to select the perfect bottle of wine for a pasta dinner—and if not for his support she probably would have returned to Des Moines a long time ago.

"Ms. Sharpe has been preparing for your meeting for several days now, and she's anxious to tell you about the charities we support here at LA Marketing Enterprises."

"I'm happy to hear that, sir." Dante put on his sunglasses, and took his keys out of his pocket. "It's been a pleasure speaking with you, and I look forward to doing it again soon."

Pride covered his fleshy face. "Thank you, Mr. Morretti. I'd like that very much."

"I'm ready when you are, Ms. Sharpe. Shall we go?"

A giggle tickled Jordana's throat.

"Do whatever it takes to impress him." Mr. Lundqvist spoke just loud enough for her to hear. "And don't come back until you have a sizable donation. Understood?"

Chapter 4

"Two visits in two days? To what do I owe this honor?"

Dante opened the glass door, and stepped aside to let Jordana exit the building. Outside, there were more luxury cars in the streets than pedestrians on the sidewalk, and the air held the scent of rain. A helicopter buzzed overhead, and clouds drifted across the somber gray sky. It was the perfect day to be home, watching movies in bed, but since hanging out with Dante was the next best thing, Jordana fell into step beside him.

"You didn't give me much of a choice. Yesterday you said I owed you lunch, so I freed up some time in my schedule, and here I am."

"Dante, I was kidding. Picking Matteo up from school was my pleasure, not a chore."

"I know. That's why I wanted to do something nice for you."

"And why you tricked my boss," she added, with a knowing smile.

"Mr. Lundqvist was ranting and raving when I walked in, but when I told him about our meeting he whooped for joy." Dante chuckled. "I think I even saw a tear in his eye!"

Walking down the street, talking and cracking jokes, Jordana felt her worries subside and her mood brighten. As suspected, he'd charmed her supervisor and concocted a convincing tale to win her freedom. Jordana was happy to be out of the office. Going out for lunch was a hundred times better than eating last night's leftovers in the windowless staff room, and she always had a good time with Dante. "How's my favorite four-year-old doing?"

"Matteo's great." Love shone in his eyes, brightening his face. "He's spending the night tomorrow, and I have tons of activities planned for Sunday afternoon. You should join us."

"I can't. Waverly and I are having a girls' day, and she'll kill me if I cancel."

"Why? What are you guys doing? Robbing a bank, Thelma and Louise style?"

"Not this weekend," she quipped, with a laugh. "We're checking out the Cinco de Mayo celebration at Griffith Park, then enjoying a Jennifer Lopez movie marathon at home."

Dante made a face. "A Jennifer Lopez movie marathon? Sounds painful."

"You're all talk! I bet if J. Lo walked past us right now you'd be all over her."

"Damn right I would! Baby's got back!"

Giggling, she playfully jabbed him in the ribs with her elbow. Being with Dante helped her forget her problems—at least momentarily. He made her feel alive, downright giddy. It had been that way from the moment they had met. Dante was an influential businessman who rubbed shoulders with the rich and famous, but he never made her feel less than. They were polar opposites, but he'd always been there for her, and she valued his friendship.

"This way," he said, taking her gently by the arm. "I'm parked around the corner."

Jordana flicked a finger in the air, gestured to the cafés and restaurants lining the streets. "Let's eat around here. I only have an hour for lunch, and I don't want to waste time sitting in traffic, listening to you talk about how amazing your new sports car is."

"That's cold, but since you brought it up, did I tell you my Porsche Spyder has overhead airbags, heated seats and chrome wheels?"

"Please. I know nothing about cars, and I don't want to learn, so spare me!"

"Is that any way to talk to the guy who rescued you from your overbearing boss?" A grin dimpled his cheek, and his lips had never looked more tempting. Hooking an arm around her waist, he pulled her close and tapped a finger against his cheek. "I think you owe me a kiss, so plant one right here."

A shiver danced down her spine. Cocky but likable, Dante was the kind of guy most fathers warned their daughters to stay away from, but his confidence was a turn-on. Jordana would never act on her feelings, even if he made a move on her, and besides, he was still carrying a torch for his ex-wife. He denied it, said he didn't love Lourdes anymore, but a blind man could see the truth. "It's a good thing I like you or I'd be running in the opposite direction!" she joked, giving him a peck on the cheek. "Happy now?"

Winking, he patted her hips good-naturedly. "Immensely."

"Can we eat now? I'm so hungry I'm having double vision!"

You're not dizzy because you're hungry, her inner voice said matter-of-factly. *You're dizzy because of Dante's smile.*

Her head was spinning, and her heart was beating out

of control. *What's the matter with me? Why am I breathless? And why am I staring at Dante's mouth, wishing it was between my—*

"What are you in the mood for?"

You mean besides you, in my bed, slathered in chocolate?

Jordana told herself to knock it off, to quit making *eyes* at him. She hadn't been intimate with anyone in a very long time, but she didn't miss sex. Not in the least. That's why her physical reaction to Dante—a guy who was like a brother to her—was shocking. Her breathing was shallow, her erect nipples strained against her bra, and the urge to kiss him was all she could think about. "I'm not fussy. You pick."

They decided on an American-style restaurant, three blocks from LA Marketing Enterprises, and picked a table in front of the window. People-watching was one of Jordana's favorite activities, had been since she was a child. As she sat down, she spotted a reality star exiting a high-end boutique. Having met dozens of A-listers over the years, Dante didn't care who was causing a frenzy outside but Jordana couldn't resist whipping out her iPhone and snapping away. For as long as she could remember, she'd always dreamed of being an actress. Her parents, namely her father, thought she was delusional, wasting her precious time chasing stardom. But she was determined to prove him wrong. Pleased with the photographs, she dropped her cell phone into her tote bag and picked up the glossy, laminated menu.

The decor was simple, but the heady aromas in the air made her mouth water. Hunger pangs began to stab at her stomach. Perusing the menu, Jordana decided on the quinoa soup and arugula salad. Dante teased her, said she ate like a bird, but she laughed off his comments.

"Want to share a bottle of wine?"

"No, thanks. I need a clear head this afternoon at work."

Jordana raised an eyebrow, wearing a knowing smile. "So do you, Mr. CIO."

"It's one drink. Live a little, girl."

I did, and it almost cost me my life, she thought sadly, dropping her gaze to her lap.

"Would you like to hear the day's specials?"

They placed their order with the waitress, and chatted about their workday while they waited for their entrées to arrive.

"Anything new and exciting happening in the world of real estate today?"

"Always," Dante said, nodding. "I'm working my ass off trying to broker a deal with Chinese billionaire Lu Quan. But despite my best efforts, he won't sign the contracts. When I was in Hong Kong, I wined and dined him, but to no avail."

"Then think outside the box. Do something unexpected to earn his trust."

Stroking his chin, he furrowed his brow and cocked his head to the right as if the answer he was looking for was written on the beige walls. "Like what?"

"The possibilities are endless. You live in the most exciting city in the world."

"Endless, huh? Enlighten me."

"Take him on a helicopter tour, spend the day wine tasting in Napa Valley, or invite him to your home for a traditional Italian meal with all the fixings." Jordana picked up her glass and tasted her strawberry lemonade. "Don't mention your business deal, though. Be a great host, and get to know him as a person, no strings attached."

"That's brilliant! Why didn't I think of that?"

Jordana beamed, felt proud as Dante showered her with praise and compliments. Encouraged, she offered more suggestions, and giggled when Dante reached across the table, cupped her face in his hands and kissed her on each cheek. It was all for show, to make her laugh, and she did. His cologne mingled with the aromas in the air, washed over her like a gentle mist, tickling and teasing her senses.

"How is your mom feeling? "

Jordana started to speak, but slammed her mouth shut before the truth spilled out. They were friends, sure, but she didn't feel comfortable opening up to Dante about her personal problems. Her family was a mess, had been for years, and she didn't know how to fix things, so why bother baring her soul? Still, her inner voice implored her to confide in him, to seek his advice, so she swallowed her pride and asked the question dominating her thoughts. "Hey, you're a real estate guy," she said, trying to sound casual. "Any tips on how to stop a home foreclosure? My mom got a letter from the bank today, and she's freaking out."

He moved closer and draped an arm around the back of her chair. "Jordana, what's going on, and why didn't you tell me your mom was having financial troubles?"

His tone irked her, grated on her nerves. He looked pissed, as if she'd personally offended him, but Jordana kept her cool. Thanks to Dante, she was out for lunch, instead of stuck in her cubicle, contemplating how to fake her own death, and that was reason enough not to get mad at him for yelling at her. "Why are you mad?"

"Because we're friends. If you need something you should come to me first."

His words troubled her, made her feel guilty for letting him down, which was an odd reaction considering they weren't lovers.

"Start from the beginning, and tell me everything."

Jordana did, but it wasn't enough. He questioned her about the house, the balance of the mortgage, the payment history and even her mother's credit score. Opening up to Dante was therapeutic. She told him things she'd never shared with anyone, not even her girlfriends. "My mom's had financial problems for as long as I can remember, but I didn't realize how dire things were until she called me this morning in tears." Jordana stared at her hands, twisted and turned her fingers. "My parents were never legally married, so my mom raised me and my brothers without much help from my dad."

"It must have been hard for her to raise three children on her own."

"That's the understatement of the year." It was hell, but Jordana kept the truth to herself. Dante didn't need to know about the month they were homeless, the nights she went to bed hungry, or their weekly visits to the food bank. No one did. It was embarrassing, something Jordana never talked about, and just thinking about her childhood made her heart ache with pain.

"How did your mom manage?" His smile and his tone were sympathetic. "Housekeepers don't make much, and kids are expensive."

"She did what any good mom would do. She worked hard, sacrificed and put the needs of her children above her own."

Reaching inside his jacket pocket, he took out a leather-bound checkbook and a gold pen speckled with diamonds. "How much do you need?"

"Dante, I can't take your money."

"I thought you wanted to save your mom's house?"

"I do, but I want to do it my way, with my resources."

"But we're friends," he argued, anger evident in his curt tone. "Why is it so hard for you to accept my help?"

Because the last time I put my faith in someone I got burned, and I won't be fooled again.

"You can pay me back when it's convenient for you," he continued. "No pressure."

"I appreciate the offer, but no, thanks. If you have any other suggestions that don't require me owing you thousands of dollars for the rest of my life I'm all ears."

The waitress arrived, carrying a wooden tray, and set it down on the table. She unloaded the entrées, her eyes glued to Dante's face. She stared at him with longing, and made no attempt to hide her desire. "I hope you enjoy your meal, Mr. Morretti, and if you need anything just let me know."

Dante gave a polite nod, then picked up his napkin and draped it across his lap.

Beaming, the waitress left, swishing her hips as she sashayed through the dining room.

"She knows your name," Jordana said, smirking. "You must eat here a lot."

"This is my first time here." Dante picked up his utensils and forked a baby potato into his mouth. He chewed slowly, as if savoring the taste, then shrugged a shoulder. "She probably saw the feature in *LA Business* magazine, and figured she'd get a huge tip if she's extra nice."

"Then she thought wrong, because it's my treat and I'm not a Morretti millionaire!"

His frown returned, and Jordana wondered what she'd done wrong this time.

"Your treat? No way. You're not paying the bill. Not today, not ever."

"Dante, it's not the fifteen hundreds."

He cocked an eyebrow. "What's that supposed to mean?"

"I work, too, so you don't have to pick up the tab every time we go out—"

"Yes, I do."

"Why?" she demanded, annoyed that he was arguing with her about something so trivial.

A devilish grin claimed his mouth, making him look sexier than a cover model. His stare was as blinding as the sun. "Because I'm a perfect gentleman."

"Ha!" she quipped, with an exaggerated laugh. "No you're not. A perfect gentleman would *never* insult my cooking, so you must be an imposter."

Dante chuckled, and Jordana did, too, enjoying the lighthearted moment with him.

"I won't be an aspiring actress forever, you know. One day I'm going to be a world-famous movie star and you're going to regret the way you treated me."

"Stop calling yourself an aspiring actress." His voice was stern. "You're an actress. Period. You've been in dozens of commercials, and actively pursuing your dreams for years..."

Enthralled by the sound of his voice, she forgot about lunch, and soaked up every word that came out of his broad, sensuous mouth. Her arugula salad was dry and drowning in honey dressing, but Jordana was having such a good time with Dante she didn't complain when the waitress returned to check up on them.

"Moving to LA to follow your dreams takes guts and determination. Don't beat yourself up because you're not a household name yet."

"That's what Waverly said. It took her sister five years to find an agent, and another three years before she landed a movie role. But I hope it doesn't take that long for me because I'm starting to lose hope in the process."

"Don't." His tone was firm, convincing. "Be positive. You'll make it."

"Seriously, Dante? You really think so?"

"Absolutely. There isn't a doubt in my mind. You have *star* written all over you, and it's just a matter of time before you're discovered, and Hollywood comes calling."

Jordana wished she shared his confidence, but after countless auditions and rejections, her future seemed more uncertain than ever.

Dante's cell phone beeped. He put down his fork, picked up his iPhone and swiped a finger across the screen. "This will only take a minute."

Jordana finished her food, and then excused herself to use the ladies' room. Returning minutes later, she was surprised to find Dante still typing away on his phone. Sitting down, she stared at him, hoping he'd put the device away, but no luck. "Did you come here to have lunch with me or play on your cell?"

He glanced up from his phone. "Sorry, but Lourdes is being a pain in the ass, and if I don't put my foot down she'll think it's okay to inconvenience me whenever the mood strikes."

"Dante, don't do that."

Wrinkles furrowed his eyebrows. "Don't do what?"

"Disrespect your ex-wife. She's the mother of your child, and bashing her isn't cool," she said, noting the scowl on his lips. "What's wrong? Why are you guys fighting?"

"She wants me to pick up Matteo tonight, instead of tomorrow morning."

"Why is that a problem? Do you have plans after work?"

"No, but that's not the point. It's the principle. I don't change the schedule at the last minute, and neither should she."

Jordana shrugged. "Life happens. Things change. And considering you only see Matteo once a week you should be thrilled to spend some extra time with him."

Dante winced, and then shook his head. "I hate when you do that."

"Do what?"

"Make me feel like an ass."

"Don't thank me," she joked, winking. "It was easy!"

Dante threw his napkin at her, calling her a no-good know-it-all, and Jordana laughed.

"I better get back to the sweatshop before my boss reams me out for being late."

"Tell Mr. Lundqvist lunch was a rousing success, and that you secured a sizable donation for Saint Jude's Hospital. Tell him the check will arrive early next week."

"Thanks, Dante. Your donation, whether big or small, will help change lives."

He opened his wallet, took out a crisp hundred-dollar bill and dropped it on the table. Jordana wanted to argue, to remind him lunch was her treat, but he sent her a chilling look, one that caused the baby-fine hairs on the back of her neck to stand up.

"FYI, there's nothing more emasculating to a man than seeing a woman reach into her purse and pull out her wallet, so don't even think about it."

Dante strode around the table, pulled out Jordana's chair and helped her to her feet. Feeling his hand on her hips shouldn't have excited her but it did. His woodsy, musky cologne went straight to her head, causing her skin to tingle and her legs to wobble. Strong, take-charge types had always been her weakness, and Dante knew how to treat a woman right.

He should, said her inner voice. *He's probably had more lovers than a British boy band!*

"I'll walk you back to work."

"Do I have a choice?"

His eyes narrowed, and Jordana knew she didn't. Walking back to LA Marketing Enterprises, she told him about activities happening around the city that weekend. The Cinco de Mayo parade scheduled for next Friday, and kids movies showing at the IMAX theater.

"I don't know what I'd do without you. You always have great ideas for things to do with Matteo." Staring down at her, he flashed a broad, devilish grin. "You're a keeper, Jordana. If I'm still single at fifty, I'm going to marry you."

Jordana patted his cheek. "If you're still single at fifty you need a shrink, not a wife!" Smirking, she tossed him a wave over her shoulder, strode confidently across the street and disappeared inside her office building.

Chapter 5

Dante turned left on Sunset Plaza Drive, spotted a child standing alone on the sidewalk and frowned. Convinced he was seeing things, he shook his head, but the image remained. Leaning forward in his seat, he peered out the windshield of his Porsche. He scanned the kid from head to toe. Curly hair. Batman-themed shirt. White shorts and Nike runners. It *was* Matteo. His eyes widened in alarm, then narrowed. What the hell? Was Lourdes out of her damn mind? Why would she let Matteo play outside alone?

Gripping the steering wheel, Dante stepped on the gas. The car zoomed down the street, shot through the air at the speed of light. Lourdes lived in a quiet community teeming with mansions, sports cars and socialites, but that didn't mean the neighborhood was safe. Every day on the evening news there were stories of children being victimized and abused, and Dante didn't want his four-year-old son in harm's way. He'd never forgive himself if Matteo got hurt, and shuddered to think what would happen if his son had crossed paths with a criminal while playing alone outside. Unfortunately, Dante knew all too well how quickly life could change.

Thoughts of Lucca filled his mind, and sadness pierced his heart. Six years ago, his nephew died in a tragic pool accident at Emilio's Greensboro estate, and to this day his brother blamed himself for what had happened. Years later he'd found love with Sharleen Nichols, a bubbly, effervescent life coach who'd helped him overcome his grief. But the accident had changed Emilio forever, and Dante didn't want his family to suffer the loss of another child. Lourdes accused him of being overprotective, of "babying" Matteo, but he didn't care what she thought. He knew what was best for their son, and this time he wasn't backing down.

Dante parked on the cobblestone driveway, and threw open his door. He scooped Matteo up in his arms, and hugged him tight. "Hey, little man. What are you doing?"

"Collecting rocks. I'm going to build a fort."

"Where's your mom?"

"On the phone with her boyfriend."

Which one? he thought sourly. Since their divorce, Lourdes had dated one man after another, including several of his business rivals. Dante didn't care what she did, or rather *whom* she did, as long as she took good care of his son. Though he suspected she was spending more time with her suitors than with Matteo, and that didn't sit well with him. "Ready to go?" Dante asked.

"Can we go to the zoo? I want to see the elephants and hippos."

"Not today. Daddy has work to do tonight, so we're going to hang out at the house."

"Please," he whined, clasping his hands together. "I promise to be on my best behavior."

Dante shook his head, refusing to even consider it. He hated public places, and just the thought of going to the

LA Zoo made him break out in hives. It was crowded and noisy, not to mention smelly. Dante could think of a million things he'd rather do on his day off. Besides, he had a mountain of paperwork waiting for him in his home office, and emails to answer before the end of the day. "Maybe next week."

"You always say that," he said, poking out his bottom lip. "When are we going to do something I want to do? When are we going to do something fun?"

"Tomorrow, I promise. We'll go swimming, play video games and make homemade pizza for dinner. How does that sound?"

Matteo shrugged his bent shoulders, kicked a rock across the driveway.

"Let's go grab your bag."

Finding the front door unlocked, Dante pushed it open and strode inside the foyer. The scent of nicotine polluted the air. Framed photographs of Lourdes adorned the magenta walls, colorful sculptures beautified end tables, and potted plants and flowers gave the three-story house an exotic look. Walking through the main floor, in search of his ex-wife, Dante noticed shoes, toys and books strewn about, and suspected Lourdes had fired her housekeeper.

"You're late."

Dante turned, saw Lourdes propped against the breakfast bar, and wondered what he'd ever seen in her. Looking every bit a diva in full makeup, a white, off-the-shoulder blouse and skinny jeans, she sauntered into the living room on six-inch heels. Lourdes had tanned skin, dyed blond hair and, thanks to her plastic surgeon, an hourglass shape. She was twenty-eight years old, but acted like a spoiled teenager. For that reason, he had to protect his son from her, no matter what. "Matteo, Mom and Dad need to talk." Dante led his son over to the winding staircase. "Go upstairs, and grab your overnight bag."

"Okay, Dad. I'll be right back. Don't leave without me!"

Matteo ran up the stairs.

"We agreed you wouldn't smoke in the house."

Lourdes shot him a blank stare, looking at him as if he were speaking a foreign language. "*I* didn't agree to anything. This is my house, not yours, so quit bossing me around."

Dante wrinkled his nose. Lourdes wasn't stumbling around, or slurring her words, but he could smell vodka on her breath. He wondered how many drinks she'd had that morning, but he didn't ask. Fighting with her would only make things worse, so he stuck to the matter at hand.

"I'm getting sick and tired of you telling me what to do."

"Then act like a responsible adult and I won't have to."

"You can be such a jerk sometimes. I don't know what I ever saw in you—"

"Secondhand smoke can lead to serious health problems in children, like asthma, depression and even behavioral and cognitive issues," he said, calling to mind an article he'd once read on the subject. "I don't want Matteo to suffer because of your poor choices."

"You smoke cigars," she shot back, her eyes bright with triumph.

"Socially, yes, but I've never lit up in front of Matteo, and I never will."

"Same here. I'd never do anything to put Matteo in harm's way."

Dante wanted to grab Lourdes and shake some sense into her, but he exercised restraint. They both knew she was lying, so why waste his time fighting with her? It wouldn't solve anything, and would only make him more upset. "I don't want Matteo playing outside alone… It…" Thoughts of Lucca bombarded his mind, and Dante faltered over his words. "It isn't safe. Anything could happen."

"You're being paranoid," she said, with a dismissive wave of her hand. "He's fine."

Angry, Dante tapped the side of his head with his index finger. "Don't you ever think? Someone could grab Matteo, in the blink of an eye, and you wouldn't know because you're in the house yapping on your stupid cell phone."

"That's not going to happen. We live in one of the best communities in LA, and everyone looks out for each other. Besides, nothing bad ever happens in West Hollywood."

"How would you know? You don't watch the news."

"Just because I don't watch CNN 24/7 doesn't mean I don't know what's going on in the world. I do. I'm very informed—"

"Social media isn't a credible news source."

"I'm sick of this," she spat, stomping her feet.

That makes two of us, Dante thought. *If not for Matteo I'd have nothing to do with you.*

"I can't wait to move to Boston, and there's nothing you can do to stop me."

Stop you? Are you kidding me? I'll help you pack! He'd need help with Matteo, and wondered if his mom would be willing to come to LA for a few months. If not, he'd hire Jordana to be a live-in nanny. She'd babysat Matteo countless times before, and treated him like her own.

"When are you leaving?" he asked, struggling to control his excitement.

"By the end of the summer."

Dante wanted to jump in the air, and click his heels together, but wisely kept his feet on the ground. It was the best news he'd heard all week, hell, all month, and he couldn't wait to move Matteo—and Jordana—into his estate. The thought of her living under his roof made him sweat under the collar. He imagined them kissing, ripping off each other's clothes, and envisioned them making love in every inch of his Bel Air mansion.

An erection stabbed the zipper of his pants. Dante blinked, striking the explicit image from his mind. Hooking up with Jordana was out of the question, and if he wanted to keep their friendship intact, he had to stop fantasizing about her.

"I can't believe you're okay with this. My attorney said you'd haul me back to court."

"Why would I do that? You're free to do as you please."

"As if! You flipped out when I took Matteo with me to Sacramento for my family reunion, so I thought you'd have a stroke when I told you we're moving to Boston…"

We? His eyes flew open and his jaw dropped. Her words echoed in his mind. It hurt to breathe, to think. Matteo couldn't move! His life was in LA, and he wasn't letting Lourdes take him away. "What's in Boston?"

"I'm dating someone and things are getting serious."

His lips thinned, and he spoke through clenched teeth. "I won't let you take my son."

"You can't stop me."

"You can't move to the East Coast. I'll never see Matteo."

"You're *so* dramatic," she said, rolling her eyes. "You can see Matteo as often as you like. You have access to a private plane. Hell, buy your own jet. You're filthy rich!"

Her response annoyed him, only made him angrier. Then it hit him. What Lourdes was doing. She was playing him—again. His ex-wife wasn't moving to the East Coast. She loved LA, would tell anyone who'd listen how great her hometown was and hated cold weather with a passion. This was about money. Plain and simple. Had to be. Convinced he was right, he decided to play his hunch. "What will it take to change your mind?"

Her face lit up. "I'm a reasonable person. I'm sure we can work something out."

"How much?" he pressed. Dante wished he had his cell

phone, so he could record their conversation. Lourdes was blackmailing him, essentially holding his son hostage. But without proof, it would be his word against hers, and his accusations would never hold up in court.

"I could cool my heels for five hundred thousand."

Dante felt weak, as if he'd been sucker punched in the gut. For years, he'd suspected that Lourdes had never loved him—just his bank account—and realized how stupid he'd been. He never should have married her, never should have given her his heart, or his last name.

"Do we have a deal?"

"I'll think about it."

"What's there to think about? Do you want to see your son or not?"

Matteo burst into the room, and Dante stared at his pride and joy. He'd never known true love until Matteo was born, and counted his birth as the happiest day of his life. He'd spent hours beside his tiny bassinet, watching over him, and the morning he'd brought Matteo home from the hospital he'd promised to be a good father. He wasn't perfect, and he still had a lot to learn, but Matteo was his number one priority, and that would never change.

"Daddy, let's go! I'm hungry."

"Where do you think you're going?" Lourdes frowned, and propped her hands on her hips. "Are you leaving with my hugs and kisses? Come here!"

Lourdes picked up Matteo, and smothered his face in kisses. He shrieked, giggled until tears streamed down his cheeks. Dante was ready to go, he couldn't stand to spend another second in his ex-wife's presence, but he didn't interrupt. His ex-wife was the most conniving person he'd ever met, but Matteo loved her, and he'd never do anything to disrespect her. He wasn't moved by her outpouring of love and affection. It was an act. If she loved Matteo, as she said she did, she'd never do anything to hurt him. And, more often than not, she had.

"Dad, I'm ready."

Matteo clasped his hand, squeezed it, and his heart melted. Walking back through the foyer, holding his son in his arms, he felt his anger subside and his mood improve. Deciding his paperwork could wait, he opened the car, buckled Matteo into his booster seat and said, "Let's go to the zoo. I want to see the elephants and hippos. Do you?"

Matteo cheered, said he was the best dad ever, and Dante felt ten feet high.

"Dad, hurry up. The animals are waiting, and I don't want to be late."

Dante chuckled, but as he drove down the street, the heaviness in his chest returned. *I'm moving to Boston... I'm taking Matteo... You can't stop me...* Lourdes's words played in his mind, taunting him like a schoolyard bully. He glanced in the rearview mirror, saw Matteo playing with his WWE action figures, and wore a sad smile. Dante didn't know what his legal rights were, but he knew one thing for sure: he wasn't losing his son.

Dante rolled the dough into a ball, and then dropped it on the granite countertop. He wiped his hands along his apron, turned on the oven and set the timer for fifteen minutes. Rapping the lyrics to the song playing on the satellite radio, he grabbed his supplies from the cupboard and set them on the breakfast bar. "Matteo, get in here. I need your help."

"But I'm playing on my iPad!"

"Do you want pizza for dinner or not?"

Matteo raced into the kitchen, hopped on the stepping stool in front of the sink and washed his hands. Together, they cut the Italian sausage, pineapple chunks and pepperoni into thin slices. Using a rolling pin, they flattened the dough until it was smooth and round. To make Matteo laugh, Dante tossed the dough in the air, and caught it behind his back.

"Wow, Dad, that was cool!" he gushed, his eyes wide and bright. "Do it again!"

Dante dropped the dough on the pan, and sprinkled Italian herbs on it. "Your turn."

"I can't remember what comes next." Matteo scratched his head. "Is it the sauce?"

"Yes, then the toppings," he instructed, gesturing to the ceramic bowls. "And don't scrimp on the cheese. I just *love* mozzarella."

Matteo giggled, punched him in the shoulder, and Dante laughed, too.

Ten minutes later, they put the pizza in the oven, cleaned the counter and swept the floor.

"Dad, can I call Mom again?"

"Be patient, li'l man. She'll call you back when she's free."

"Okay," he said, shoving his hands into the pockets of his shorts. "Can I ride my bike?"

"We've been outside in the hot sun all day. Aren't you tired?"

Matteo shook his head. "No. I want to ride my bike to the ice-cream store."

"Cool your heels, son. Your dad's old, and he needs a break!"

They'd spent the afternoon at the Los Angeles Zoo and Botanical Gardens, and as expected, the crowd was thick, the lines long and the noise deafening. For hours, they'd wandered from one exhibit to the next, feeding animals, taking pictures and snacking on junk food. He'd texted Jordana to join them, but she had an audition on Monday for a TV movie, and was busy practicing her lines with a friend. They'd been texting all day, trading messages back and forth, but Dante wanted to see her. Talking to Jordana always made him feel better, and he needed someone to vent to about his argument with Lourdes. Maybe tomorrow on their way to Zuma Beach, they'd swing by for a short visit, he thought.

His cell phone buzzed. Glancing at it, he realized he had eight new emails, and groaned in frustration. On the drive home from the zoo, Matteo had dozed off, and Dante had called his assistant to touch base. There were several matters that required his immediate attention, and just thinking about everything he had to do made his head pound.

The timer went off, and Dante broke free of his thoughts. Opening the oven, he took the metal pan from the rack and then closed the door with the back of his foot. The air was inundated with the scent of oregano, and the mouthwatering aroma made him salivate.

"Uncle Markos!"

Matteo shot across the kitchen, and threw himself into his uncle's arms. Watching his son goofing around with his eldest brother made Dante reflect on his childhood. He grew up knowing his parents loved him, and he wanted the same for his son. To him, family mattered more than anything, but his ex-wife obviously didn't feel the same way. It angered him that she put others before their son. Matteo had been calling her all day, and she had yet to call him back. Dante was frustrated, and made up his mind to discuss his legal options with Markos about it. He needed to be there for his son, now more than ever, and he was ready to step up to the plate.

"Did you bring me something?"

"You know it!" Like a magician, with a flair for the dramatic, Markos reached behind Matteo's ear and pulled out a five-dollar bill. "Looking for this?"

Matteo cheered. "Do it again, Uncle, but this time make a hundred-dollar bill appear!"

Chuckling, Dante greeted his brother with a nod. Though casually dressed in a button-down shirt, khaki shorts and leather sandals, Markos carried himself with the air of a king, and exuded power and masculinity. At six foot six, he was the tallest person in the Morretti family, and according to his ex-wife, the most intimidating. "What's up, man?"

"Nothing," he answered, putting Matteo down on the floor. "Is dinner ready?"

"I just took it out of the oven."

"Good, because I'm starving and I'm sick of eating Chinese takeout."

"I wasn't expecting to see you tonight." Dante opened the utensil drawer, and grabbed the pizza cutter. "I thought you were going to the symphony."

"And miss out on spending time with my favorite nephew? Hell no!"

"Kara canceled on you again, huh?"

"It's all good. I didn't want to go to the symphony anyway, so I gave the tickets to a client." Speaking with bravado, as if he didn't have a care in the world, he opened the fridge and grabbed a beer. "Besides, I'd much rather hang out here with you and Matteo than listen to Kara wax poetic about her amazing new boss and his impressive yacht collection."

"Don't sweat it, bro. It's her loss."

"Damn right it is. I'm one hell of a catch."

To make him laugh, Dante clapped him good-naturedly on the shoulder, and winked. "Keep telling yourself that and maybe one day she'll believe you, too!"

Markos chuckled, but it sounded forced. Dante could tell by his dark gaze and the solemn expression on his face that he *was* upset his date had canceled at the last minute. Of all his brothers, Markos was the most sensitive, and although Dante teased him for wearing his heart on his sleeve, he admired him greatly. Markos was smart, perceptive and well-read, and he could always count on him to listen to his problems, and give him sound advice. These days, he felt as if Markos was all he had. Now that Emilio and Immanuel had found love, Dante rarely saw them, and he couldn't recall the last time he'd talked to Romeo or Enrique. They rarely traveled to the States, and teased him endlessly for having a "day job." Their guys-only trip to Tampa was fast approaching and he was looking forward to hanging out with his brothers and cousins. The vacation was long overdue, and he couldn't wait to see his family.

"Dad, can I eat in the living room? I want to watch *Teenage Mutant Ninja Turtles*."

He thought of Jordana and the showdown they'd had in her apartment days earlier, and smiled to himself. If she was there she'd give him an earful for even considering Matteo's request, but since it was his house, and he wanted to talk privately with Markos, he said, "Sure, li'l man, but be careful. Don't spill anything."

"I won't." Matteo picked up his plate, and raced out of the room. "Thanks, Dad!"

"Can I eat in the living room, too? I promise not to spill my beer on the carpet."

Dante picked up the pizza pan, and set it down on the kitchen table. "Sit your ass down. We need to talk and I don't want Matteo to hear us."

Markos grabbed a slice of Hawaiian pizza, sprinkled Parmesan cheese on it and folded it in half like a club sandwich. "Sounds serious, bro. What's going on?"

Thinking about his argument with Lourdes that afternoon made his blood boil again, but Dante spoke calmly. He told Markos about Ms. Papadopoulos's frantic phone call on Wednesday, and his subsequent conversations with his ex-wife. "I don't know what to do," he confessed, feeling the weight of the world on his shoulders. "Lourdes is more interested in finding Mr. Right than taking care of Matteo, and I'm worried about his well-being."

"Then file for shared custody."

"I don't want shared custody. I want full custody."

Markos raised an eyebrow. "That's going to be a tough sell, bro. The only way the court will give you full custody is if you prove Lourdes is an unfit mother."

"I don't have to prove anything. She is!"

"There's something else you can do, but I know you'll never go for it."

"What?" he asked, intrigued. "Tell me. I'll do anything to win custody."

"Get married."

Dante barked a laugh. "Are you insane? Why would I do something crazy like that?"

"Because it works. The courts want to see children in a stable environment, and since a two-parent home is still the ideal, tying the knot will work in your favor."

"Hell no! I hated being married, and I won't do it again."

"You'll be married only on paper, and once you win custody you can have it annulled and no one will ever be the wiser." Markos stood, walked over to the stove and helped himself to three more slices of pizza. "There are no guarantees in life, but it's worth a try."

"It will never work."

"It can and it will. Trust me. I've seen it all, and then some, during my ten years of practicing law. The marriage-for-custody scheme works more often than not."

Dante still wasn't convinced. "I think it's a stupid idea. And how do you propose I go about finding a bride? On TemporaryWife.com?"

"No, for the ruse to work you'll have to marry someone you already know, or the court will doubt your love story." Markos took a bite of his pizza. "Why don't you marry

Elizabeth? She's had a thing for you ever since you hired her, and she'd probably love playing your wife."

Dante shook his head, refusing to entertain the suggestion. "No way. She's the best assistant I've ever had, and I'd like to keep it that way. Besides, her on-again, off-again boyfriend is a mixed martial arts champion, and I don't want to get my ass kicked if things go south."

Markos stroked the length of his jaw for several seconds, then snapped his fingers. "Marry Jordana. She's single, hot as hell, and she adores Matteo."

Dante stared at his brother as if he'd taken leave of his senses. Jordana's heart belonged to another man—his college buddy—and he didn't want to upset Tavares, or lose his friendship.

His thoughts returned to Valentine's Day. He remembered how much fun they'd had at Epic Bar and Lounge talking and laughing, and how good it had felt holding her in his arms slow dancing to the live band. Jordana would make a fantastic wife, and an even better mother. He could see them now. Goofing around in the kitchen. Swimming in the backyard. Going on day trips to her favorite hangouts. She'd look great on his arm at charity events and business functions. "I can't believe I'm actually considering this harebrained scheme," Dante confessed, speaking his thoughts aloud. "It's crazy."

"Do you want custody or not?"

His gaze zeroed in on his son. Matteo looked happy, and hearing him giggle made Dante smile. "Are you sure about this?"

"Have I ever steered you wrong before?"

Now it was Dante's turn to laugh out loud. "Yeah, for the record, you have!"

"I know several celebrities who've used this strategy, and more often than not it worked," Markos explained, his expression serious, and his tone matter-of-fact. "If I were you I'd…"

His cell phone rang, but Dante didn't answer. It could wait. All ears, he leaned forward in his chair, listening intently to what his brother had to say. An idea he'd been toying with for weeks came to mind. "Do you still have friends in the LAPD?"

"Yeah, why?"

"Find out if any of your buddies on the force want to make some extra cash."

"I'll do it now." Markos put down his beer, and picked up his cell phone.

Mulling over everything they'd discussed, Dante realized the answer to his problems was staring him in the face. No more Mr. Nice Guy. It was time he fight fire with fire. He didn't want Matteo moving thousands of miles away. The thought of being apart from his son filled him with anguish. Matteo was his heart, his most prized possession, and he'd do anything to win custody. If that meant playing dirty, so be it.

Chapter 6

Jordana entered her kitchen on Sunday morning, saw Waverly and her boyfriend, Rory Sutherland, playing tonsil hockey against the fridge, and lost her appetite. Their moans and groans bounced off the ceiling and ricocheted off the paper-thin walls, piercing her eardrum. It was too early for an X-rated make-out session, but they tore at each other's pajamas as if they were consumed with lust. Jordana couldn't relate. She'd never been in love, and didn't put much faith in men or romantic relationships.

To make her presence known, Jordana opened a cupboard, grabbed a mug and slammed the door shut. They didn't budge. Didn't acknowledge her. Continued fondling each other. Annoyed she couldn't get inside the fridge, she grabbed a banana from the basket on the counter and left the kitchen. Jordana thought of returning to her bedroom, but she was tired of being cooped up inside staring at the ceiling, and needed a change of scenery.

Standing against the window, she surveyed the busy

street. Kids played soccer on the weed-infested lawn, dog lovers walked their canine friends up the block, and cyclists sped through the apartment complex.

"Rory, stop… I need to eat something before round two."

Jordana wrinkled her nose. *Enough already*, she thought, casting a glance over her shoulder at the horny lovebirds. *I live here, too!* The apartment wasn't big enough for two people, let alone three. Although Jordana liked Rory, she didn't want him around 24/7. Just yesterday, she'd talked to Waverly about his daily visits, but with no success. Her roommate wasn't receptive to what she had to say, had shrugged off her concerns. To keep the peace, Jordana didn't argue, but she was tired of Rory eating her food, monopolizing the TV and leaving the toilet seat up. Then there were the outrageous noises he made in bed. In the heat of the moment, he cooed, grunted and, at times, squawked so loud Jordana thought there were pigeons in the apartment. She hadn't had a good night's sleep in days, not since he'd showed up unannounced on Wednesday evening, and Jordana was starting to feel like a third wheel in her own apartment.

"Hey, roomie. I didn't notice you standing there."

Of course you didn't, she thought sourly. *You're too busy groping your boyfriend!*

"How did you sleep?"

"Fine," Jordana answered, trying not to let her frustration show. "You?"

Waverly wrapped her arms around Rory's waist, and spoke in a girlie, high-pitched voice. "Isn't it obvious? I always sleep great when my Pooh bear spends the night."

It took everything in Jordana not to gag. In recent weeks, Waverly had discussed moving in with Rory, but Jordana knew it was all talk. Her roommate would soon get bored with the construction worker and move on to the next guy. She changed boyfriends as often as she changed her hairstyle—at least once a month—and she loved playing the field. "Are we still on for brunch, and the Cinco de Mayo festivities at Griffith Park?"

Gazing longingly at Rory, Waverly shrugged and gave an absent wave of her hand. "Yeah, sure, we'll be ready to go by noon."

We? Jordana thought, raising an eyebrow. *When did you start speaking French?*

"Make that one o'clock." Rory flashed a dirty smile, and slapped Waverly's butt. "We have some unfinished business to take care of in the bedroom, if you know what I mean."

Disappointed, she felt heaviness in her chest. All week, she'd been looking forward to having some girl time with Waverly. Outside of work, they rarely saw each other, and she missed hanging out with her friend. *What now? Should I stay home or go to the Cinco de Mayo celebration alone?* It was her day off, and she didn't want to spend it watching Waverly and Rory play kissy face all over the apartment. Not if she could help it. Jordana wondered what Dante was doing, and made up her mind to call him after she had breakfast.

Hearing her iPhone ring, she rushed down the hall and into her bedroom. Framed paintings covered the walls, keepsakes beautified the dresser and glass vases, overflowing with tulips, filled the air with their fragrant scent. Jordana swiped her cell off the desk, checked the number on the screen and put it to her ear. "Great timing," she said, flopping down on her canopy bed. "I was *just* thinking about you."

"That's good to hear, because I was thinking about you too. Hence, why I called."

"What's up? What are your plans for…"

Trailing off, her gaze strayed to the door. It was times

like this, when Waverly and Rory were all over each other in the living room, that Jordana wished she had a special man in her life. Someone she could talk to and laugh with and cook for. She wasn't jealous of Waverly, but she envied her relationship, and secretly longed to have a loving, caring boyfriend of her own.

Jordana thought about her ex and their bitter breakup. If things had gone differently she'd be a wife now, maybe even a mother. But her ex had chosen his career over her, and months later Jordana still wondered what could have been. Sure, Tavares had never given her butterflies, but he'd treated her well and she loved his small, close-knit family. She still talked to his mother, and once a month they met for lunch in Beverly Hills. "What are you and Matteo up to today?"

"We're going to Zuma Beach to fly kites," he said. "I know you're busy with Waverly today, doing fun girls' stuff, but Matteo wants to see you, and so do I."

"My plans fell through, so we can definitely meet up later."

"Or we could pick you up, and you could spend the day with us."

Footsteps pounded on the tile floor, fast and loud, and Jordana knew Rory was chasing Waverly around the apartment again. She wondered what had gotten into them, and why they were acting like five-year-olds. They were a young, fun couple who had a great time together, but they were also annoying as hell, and Jordana needed a break from their shenanigans. "Count me in!" she said, jumping to her feet. "How soon can you get here?"

"Are we there yet?" Dante heard the question leave his mouth, saw Jordana snicker, and scolded himself for sounding like a whiny, snot-nosed kid. They'd spent the morning at Zuma Beach, and he was drained. He was so damn tired all he could think about was going home, dropping into his leather arm chair and guzzling down an ice-cold beer. For hours, they'd built sand castles, flown kites and played soccer. As they were leaving the beach, Jordana had mentioned the Cinco de Mayo celebration at Griffith Park, and to his dismay Matteo had asked if they could attend the event. He'd had no choice but to swallow his protests and drive to his son's favorite park.

They'd been walking for the past fifteen minutes, searching for the "perfect" spot, and Dante feared if he didn't sit down soon he'd collapse from exhaustion. Sweat dripped from his brow, coursed down his face, drenching his blue Nike T-shirt. The sun was blinding, but he didn't complain. Jordana and Matteo were having the time of their lives, cheering and dancing, and he didn't want to ruin the festive mood. He had work to do, piles of it sitting on the desk in his home office, but it would have to wait. As Jordana so aptly pointed out minutes earlier, nothing was more important than spending quality time with his son. Dante agreed. "All the picnic tables are taken," he pointed out.

Jordana nodded. "You're right. Let's sit under the trees, so we'll have some shade."

Relieved, Dante sat down on the grass, and popped open the cooler. He grabbed a soda and guzzled it down. Sweet and cold, it was the perfect antidote for the sweltering heat. He quickly finished it and helped himself to another drink.

His gaze then zeroed in on Jordana's pretty face. She looked like a movie star in her black floppy hat, sunglasses and yellow dress. His eyes slid down her body, admiring her delicious curves. Watching her dance made his mouth wet and his temperature rise.

"LA, are you ready to party?" the female emcee shouted, gripping the microphone with one hand and cupping her ear with the other. "I can't hear you!"

The crowd screamed, whistled and cheered.

"Coming to the stage is an electrifying group who got their start right here in East LA. Give it up for the pride of El Sereno, the Mexican Folklore Dancers..."

Dante glanced up from his drink. Women in vibrant traditional dresses twirled wildly around the stage, clapping their hands and stomping their feet. In all the years he'd lived in LA he'd never attended a Cinco de Mayo celebration, and to his surprise the festival wasn't just an excuse for college students to get drunk. There were food carts and music, flamboyant costumes and activities for people of all ages. The mood was festive, the audience loud and excited, and the air held a tantalizing aroma.

"I *love* Mexican music," Jordana said, swiveling her hips to the music.

And I love watching you, he thought. *You're sexy as hell and you don't even realize it.*

"You're not going to make me dance alone, are you?" Sashaying toward him, she smiled and beckoned him over with a wave of her hands. "Come on. Just one dance."

"I'll pass. Dancing isn't my thing, but you go right ahead."

"Dante, don't be silly. Now get up."

Matteo giggled. "Come on, Dad. Don't be a party pooper!"

"Live in the moment," she advised, her smile bright and brilliant. "Go with the flow..."

Dante shook his head, and argued that he was too tired to move, but his pleas fell on deaf ears. Jordana and Matteo dragged him up to his feet, and forced him to join the slow-moving conga line. Following Jordana's lead, he moved in time to the beat of the music. *If my brothers could see me now they'd die laughing*, he thought, scouring the crowd to ensure no one was recording him with a cell phone. The last thing he needed was for a video to surface online.

"This is so much fun!" Matteo was in seventh heaven. The joyful expression on his face made Dante feel proud, as if he'd finally done something right. He couldn't remember ever seeing his son this happy. As Matteo danced with Jordana, he realized he had to do everything in his power to keep him safe and protected.

"Viva Mexico!" the emcee shouted, waving the national flag wildly in the air.

Matteo wore an inquisitive expression on his face. "What is Cinco de Mayo?" he asked, clasping Dante's hand. "Is it like Christmas? Do kids get toys and presents?"

Before Dante could answer, Jordana spoke up. Animated and excited, she told Matteo about the victory of Mexican forces over the French army at the Battle of Puebla. As she spoke, Matteo's eyes widened and brightened with interest. "Cinco de Mayo is a day of great importance not just in the Mexican community, but all over the world. With hard work and unity, anything is possible. Never forget that, Matteo. You can do anything you set your mind to…"

Her enthusiasm was contagious, and Dante found himself hanging on her every word. His gaze zeroed in on her mouth. Sucking in a deep breath, he felt the overwhelming urge to touch her, to kiss her, to play in her lush, tight curls. His imagination ran wild, stealing his focus. Dante prided himself on being a good listener, but for the life of him he couldn't focus on what Jordana was talking about. Her silky voice aroused him, tickling the tips of his ears.

"Dad, can I play on the jungle gym?"

Feeling someone yank his arm, Dante snapped to attention. "Sure, champ, let's go."

"Yahoo!" Matteo cheered. "This is the best day ever!"

Like a rocket, he shot across the field and jumped feet-first into the sandbox.

"Boys will be boys," Dante said, with a chuckle.

"You can say *that* again. Your son's a daredevil just like you."

"Thanks. I'll take that as a compliment."

Jordana stared up at him, her expression pensive. She leaned into him, and the feel of her warm skin against his made the hairs on the back of his neck rise. For a moment, Dante thought Jordana was going to kiss him, stood there wishing, hoping, willing it to happen, but she patted his cheek instead, and flashed a knowing smile. "You're a good dad, Dante."

"That means a lot coming from you."

"Just calling it like I see it. It's obvious you adore your son, and I admire…"

Mariachi musicians walked by, strumming their instruments, and a group of silver-haired women trailed behind them, cheering and clapping. Jordana broke off speaking, and Dante suspected she was thinking about her mother. "How's your mom? Have you spoken to her?"

"I spoke to her last night, but only for a few minutes. She's still pretty emotional."

"Jordana, my offer still stands."

"I appreciate it, Dante, really, I do, but I don't accept handouts. That's just not me."

"You need to change your way of thinking. It's not a handout. It's one friend helping another." To get through to her, he opened up about a painful chapter in his life. "After college, I couldn't *buy* a job and if not for the financial support of my family I would have been homeless."

She slowly nodded, as if she was mulling over his words, and toyed with the silver chain around her neck. Dante glanced at the playground, spotted Matteo swinging wildly on the monkey bars and decided this was the perfect time to talk to Jordana about his problems. Lying went against everything he believed—except when he was protecting his son. Then all bets were off. To win custody of Matteo, he was willing to break the rules, and he needed Jordana's help to carry out his plan.

"Thanks for picking me up this morning."

The sound of her voice yanked Dante out of his reverie. He looked deep into her eyes, and felt a burning sensation in his chest. His mouth was wet, and desire shot through his veins. Her floral perfume mingled with the scents in the air, tickling his nostrils. He gave his head a shake, and rested a hand on her forearm. "I have a proposition for you."

"A proposition?" Jordana turned to face him. "Sounds serious."

"You're right. *Proposition* is the wrong word. Think of it as a favor."

"Of course, another favor," she quipped, with a cheeky smile. "What is it this time? Do you need me to take Matteo to karate class tomorrow, or pick up your dry cleaning again?"

"None of the above."

"What is it?"

"I need you to be my lawfully wedded wife."

Her nose twitched, followed by the corners of her mouth. Then she burst out laughing. "Sure, buddy, anything for you. Is tomorrow soon enough? No. Why wait? Let's elope, and get hitched at a drive-through wedding chapel tonight!"

Dante swallowed the lump in his throat, the one threatening to cut off his air supply, and tasted his soda. Watching her over the rim of his can, he determined his next move. He didn't expect her to laugh in his face, and was taken aback by her response. He waited until her giggles subsided to speak. "Jordana, I'm serious. I need your help."

Her smile vanished. Sobering, she adamantly shook her head, her lush, chocolate-brown locks tumbling wildly around her face.

Dante wanted to play in her hair, imagined himself burying his hands in it and twirling her curls around his index finger. To keep from acting on his impulse, he stepped back and shoved his hands into the pocket of his shorts.

"We're friends, not lovers, so why would we do something crazy like tie the knot?"

"Because Lourdes is an unfit mother, and I want sole custody of Matteo."

"Are you out of your mind?

"You don't understand what it's like living in fear for your child."

"You're right. I don't, so tell me what's going on."

He opened up to Jordana about his tumultuous relationship with his ex. He told her about his argument with Lourdes on Friday afternoon, her blackmail attempt and his conversation with Markos last night. He saw the concern in her eyes, the sympathy, but he sensed she still wasn't on board with his plan.

"Judges consider several factors when determining custody, including the child's age, their needs and the lifestyle of each parent. If I can prove to the family court judge that I can provide a stable, loving environment for Matteo, I'll win custody."

"Dante, I can't marry you. It would be wrong and unethical."

"Unethical? In what way?"

"We don't love each other, and I won't live a lie."

"Of course I do. You're an incredible woman, and I'd do anything for you."

"You know what I mean," she said with sass, rolling her eyes. "You love me, but you're not *in* love with me. There's a big difference."

"Then think of it as a mutually beneficial business arrangement. I'll get full custody of Matteo, and you get all the perks and benefits of being Mrs. Dante Morretti." Dante touched her forearm. "At least think about it."

"There's nothing to think about."

Taking a page out of his son's playbook, he poked out his bottom lip, and clasped his hands together. "Please?" he begged. "With a cherry on top?"

"You're worse than a four-year-old," Jordana said, with a laugh. "And you wonder where Matteo gets it from."

Dante gave her a one-arm hug. "Give some thought to what I said, okay?"

"Fine, I will. Quit badgering me."

"I love you, too," he said, with a wink. "And if you help me I'll owe you big—"

"Dad, did you see me?" Matteo hurled himself into Dante's arms, and pointed at the play structure. "I raced the older kids to the water fountain, and I won!"

"Way to go, li'l man." Jordana ruffled his curls, then patted him on the back. "That calls for a celebration. How about a fruit smoothie?"

"I don't want a smoothie. I want a chocolate sundae with sprinkles, and..."

Strolling through the park, hand in hand with his son, Dante couldn't have imagined a more perfect day. The sky was clear, the sun was shining and the air held a savory aroma. But best of all, he was with his two favorite people.

Dante chanced a look at Jordana, studying her on the sly. As he did, he remembered his conversation with Immanuel weeks earlier. He'd teased him for being "whupped," and his brother had shocked him by saying, "Damn right, I'm 'whupped'! I knew Dionne was 'the one' the first time I saw her, and I wasn't letting anything—not even her insecurities—keep us apart."

Reflecting on his brother's words, an idea popped in his mind. *I know what to do!* Dante thought, his gaze narrowed in determination. He was going to take a page out of his brother's book. Failure wasn't an option, not for a Morretti. He'd have to pull out all the stops to win her over. And he would. He didn't take no for an answer—ever—not in his personal or professional life. Deep down he knew it was just a matter of time before she became his wife.

At the ice-cream vendor, Jordana and Matteo placed their orders, and Dante formulated his plan. He'd give her space, forty-eight hours to change her mind, but if he didn't hear from her by Tuesday he'd implement plan B. The next time he broached the subject, he wasn't taking no for an answer.

Chapter 7

"Guess what? Rory asked me to move in with him, and I said yes!" Beaming like a bride on her wedding day, Waverly danced into Jordana's cubicle on Tuesday afternoon, and plopped herself down on the desk. Swaying to an inaudible beat, she hugged her hands to her chest, and spoke in an awestruck voice. "Girl, he's the one. I just know it. I feel it in my bones!"

You feel it in your bones, or you like jumping *his bones?* she thought, hiding a smirk.

"You're moving to Inglewood? But you hate it more than La Brea."

Stars twinkled in her eyes. "I know, but Rory's totally worth it. He's kind and sweet and amazing in bed. What more could a girl want?"

It was a struggle to keep her temper in check, but Jordana refrained from yelling at her best friend. Waverly always had her back, was there whenever she needed her, and Jordana didn't want to rain on her parade.

"I'm moving in three days, and I can't wait"

"Three days! But we just renewed our lease."

"It's no big deal. I can transfer the lease to your name, or sublet my room," she explained, her tone bright and cheery. "Let me know what works best for you."

None of the above, Jordana thought glumly, expelling a deep breath.

"Try not to worry. Everything will work out fine—"

"That's easy for you to say. I'm not leaving *you* high and dry."

Eyes wide with surprise, her face fell, and the smile slid off her lips.

"I'm sorry," Jordana said quietly. "I shouldn't have said that."

"I thought you'd be glad I'm moving out, especially in light of our last conversation."

"I'm happy for you, but I'm worried I won't be able to pay next month's rent."

Waverly reached out, and patted her leg. "Don't stress. You'll have a new roommate in no time." She spoke in a confident tone, vigorously nodding her head. "I was sharing my good news in the staff room, and several people expressed interest in taking over my room."

Relief flooded Jordana's body. Thank God. She wasn't going to lose her apartment, or end up sleeping in a shelter. Bitter memories assailed her mind, but she pushed them aside, and made a conscious decision not to dwell on the past. "That's great," she said, wearing a grateful smile. "I'd rather live with someone I know than a stranger."

"That's what I told Archibald."

"Archibald?" Jordana wrinkled her nose, and pursed her lips. "That creepy, older guy from accounting who smells like Bengay? No way. Keep looking."

"Lee and Mohammed expressed interest as well, and so did the new security guard..."

Of course they did. They're all trying to score, but it's not *going to happen!* Like a balloon pricked with a pin, her hope deflated. Jordana fought against feelings of despair. Every time she tried to advance her acting career, life knocked her back down. *Is the universe trying to tell me something? Should I quit acting and return to Des Moines?*

Jordana shook off the thought, refusing to consider it. The fear of falling flat on her face and proving the haters wrong was her strongest motivation, and she wasn't ready to throw in the towel just yet. Her mom believed in her—Dante, too—and she didn't want to let them down, or herself. Jordana was going to make a name for herself in LA, and no one was going to stop her.

"You're too picky." Waverly wagged a finger in her face. "And you're too stubborn."

"No, I'm not. I don't feel comfortable living with a male colleague, and I don't have to."

"Fine, then use your savings to keep you afloat until you find a suitable roommate. But don't say I didn't try to help you."

What savings? Jordana thought, hanging her head. *I have to wire that money to my mom today or she'll lose her house.* Last night, after talking at length to Helene about the foreclosure letter, Jordana had swallowed her pride and called Carlito and Raymon. They were both college graduates, living and working in Des Moines, but they had nothing to do with Helene. Her mom had a long history of embarrassing their family—Jordana included—but she'd never turn her back on her. Her mom had made poor choices in the past, but didn't everyone? Why were they punishing her for being sick? Like her father, her brothers held grudges and refused to forgive. Their three-way conversation was terse, only ten minutes long. When the call ended Jordana felt a mixture of relief and anger. How dare they insult Helene? Didn't they remember all the sacrifices she'd made for their family? Didn't they care?

"I'm going to miss you."

Jordana abandoned her thoughts, and returned to the present. Touched by Waverly's words, she stood, wrapped her arms around her and pecked her rosy cheeks. "Don't be so dramatic. We'll still see each other every day at work."

"I know, but it won't be the same as living together. You're a great roommate, and an even better cook!" Exiting the cubicle, she laughed and tossed a wave over her shoulder. "I better get back to work, or Mr. Lundqvist will dock my pay again. See you at home, homie!"

Jordana laughed, but her heart was heavy with sadness. Not because Waverly had found love and was moving out but because her life was a mess, and she didn't have anyone to talk to.

Yes, you do, encouraged her inner voice. *Call Dante. He'll help you. He always does.*

Her gaze fell across her cell phone, sitting beside the box of tissues. She hadn't spoken to Dante since their outing two days earlier, and just the thought of calling him made her mouth dry and her palms sweat. Sure, they texted each other every day, but it wasn't the same as hearing his voice, and laughing with him.

Their last conversation came to mind.

I need you to be my lawfully wedded wife... If I can prove to the judge that I can provide a stable, loving environment for Matteo, I'll win custody... Please, Jordana, I need you.

Jordana reflected on his words, and gave his proposition some serious thought. Who was she kidding? They would never work. He lived a fast, fabulous lifestyle, and she'd never fit in. Furthermore, he was a control freak who had to have the last word, and she sucked at following orders. On the flip side, if she married Dante, she could save money and help her mom. Even better, she could spend quality time with Dante and Matteo. A man who'd do anything for his child was a winner in her book, and although his methods were unorthodox, she couldn't fault him for wanting to protect his son. His marriage scheme was the craziest thing she'd ever heard, so why was she even considering it? *Because I'm tired of living paycheck to paycheck.*

Jordana raised her shoulders and straightened in her chair. She didn't have time to wallow in self-pity; she had things to do. She had to wire money to her mom before her lunch break ended, and it was almost one o'clock. Pressed for time, she turned on her computer, accessed the internet and logged in to her bank account.

The numbers on the screen confused her, boggled her mind. Something wasn't right. Bewildered, Jordana rubbed her tired eyes. Nothing changed. *I haven't seen that much money in my checking account since…* Jordana paused. No, she'd *never* seen that many zeroes in her account. Scanning the week's transactions, she found the error. Yesterday, thirty-nine thousand dollars had been deposited into her account. The bank had made a mistake, she decided, drumming her fingers on her desk. *I don't know anyone with that kind of money.*

A cold chill flooded her body. Her thoughts returned to the past, to the one and only time she'd ever cursed Dante out, and just thinking about their heated argument in December made her angry all over again. Six months ago, after one too many mojitos, she'd made the mistake of telling Dante about her money troubles. Twenty-four hours later, ten thousand dollars had miraculously appeared in her checking account. Incensed, she'd stormed into his swank bachelor pad, demanding answers. Cocky as ever, he'd laughed off her concerns. He told her to keep the money, said it was her Christmas gift, and she didn't have to pay it back. Embarrassed by the handout, she'd promptly returned the money, and told him to mind his business. Mad at herself for confiding in him, she'd ignored his texts and calls for days. If not for Matteo's birthday party a week after their argument, she'd probably still be giving him the silent treatment.

Jordana seethed, felt anger course through her veins, and her hands curled into fists. Dante was doing it again. Taking over. Throwing his money around. Trying to control her. *I can't be bought! When is he going to get that through his thick skull?*

The desk phone rang. It was probably her mom, calling to find out why she hadn't transferred the money yet. If she sounded upset, her mom would worry. Snatching the receiver off the cradle, she masked her emotions by speaking in a warm, friendly tone. "Hello?"

It was the receptionist. She was talking so fast Jordana couldn't understand her.

"Come again?" she asked, pressing the receiver to her ear. "I missed that."

"You have an important visitor waiting for you in reception, so hurry down here."

"I do? Who is it? I'm not expecting anyone."

"It's someone who loves you *very* much, and they're anxious to see you."

Dread filled her stomach. *Oh, God, I hope it's not Helene!* Her mother had a history of showing up in LA unannounced. Jordana feared what would happen if her mom stormed into her office again, emotional and upset about her latest financial setback. *Will I get another warning? Or will I be fired on the spot?* Panicked, she dropped the phone on the cradle, sprang to her feet and marched briskly through the office.

Her ears perked up. The office was quiet, too quiet, and soft music was playing. It was a Celine Dion song, her favorite ballad, the only song that made her teary-eyed every time she heard it. And this afternoon was no different. Except, it was. What was going on? Where was everyone? Why were the lights suddenly dim, and the air inundated with the scent of flowers?

Jordana saw Dante standing at the end of the hall, and told herself she was dreaming. Had to be, because visitors weren't allowed on the second floor. Not even wealthy, distinguished businessmen worth millions. He was wearing a navy blue suit, tailored to perfection, and carrying the largest bouquet of red roses she'd ever seen.

Pressing her eyes shut, she counted to ten. Jordana blinked, and found that Dante was still there, staring at her with that piercing gaze of his. The real estate mogul was a force, a living, breathing wet dream, and as he crossed the room toward Jordana struggled to breathe.

"You're a dream come true," he said, in a husky voice, his boyish smile showcasing every sparkling white tooth. "Jordana, you are the only woman for me, and I want to spend the rest of my life with you..."

Stunned, her knees knocking together under her peasant dress, she cupped a hand over her mouth to trap a scream inside. Her body froze, and the room flipped upside down, spinning a hundred miles an hour. *What is Dante talking about? Is he drunk? We've never kissed. Sure, I've thought about it, fantasized about it a time or two or* ten, *but it's never happened and it never will. He's still in love with his ex-wife.*

"I love you more than I've ever loved anyone, and I want you to be my wife."

Her skin was clammy, drenched in sweat, and she shook uncontrollably.

Dante stopped in front of her, and rested the bouquet in her arms. He had the nerve to wink, as if they shared a deep, dark secret, and kissed her cheek. Jordana told herself to stay calm, not to overreact, but she was fighting mad, and wanted to wring his neck. "What are you doing?" she whispered, her eyes darting nervously around the room. "Why are you here?"

"I'm here to propose, of course."

Her tongue froze, suddenly felt too big for her mouth. She wouldn't have been more shocked if an alien had burst into the office, jumped on her desk and did the moon walk. "Propose what? I told you I'd think about it."

"Time is of the essence, so I came here to seal the deal."

Jordana refrained from rolling her eyes. To prove she meant business, she propped a hand on her hips. "Did you deposit thirty-nine thousand dollars into my bank account yesterday?"

His grin was answer enough.

"I told you I don't need your money."

"It's an early wedding present. I was going to deposit a hundred grand into your account, but I didn't want you to go off on me. You know how you get whenever I try to help you—"

"Are you crazy?"

"Yeah, baby, I'm crazy about you, and *only* you."

Jordana wanted to smack the cocksure grin off his face, but she exercised self-control. He was talking so loud everyone in the office could hear him, but she recognized it was all part of his plan. Now he had the attention of everyone in the room, her colleagues, her boss, the potbellied security guard vying to be her new roommate. Her friends were giggling and waving, but Jordana didn't find anything funny about Dante's impromptu proposal at LA Marketing.

"I promise to love you, cherish you and protect you for as long as I live. Baby, you've made my life complete, and I can't live without you." Dante took her left hand in his, and dropped to one knee. He was holding a ring between two fingers. The heart-shaped diamond was brighter than a million stars. "Jordana, will you marry me?"

Applause, shrieks of joy and whistles filled the office. Waverly was crying, her boss was cheering, and three male staffers were chanting Dante's name with zeal. The noise was deafening, so loud Jordana felt as if she was at the Staples Center amid eighteen thousand screaming fans. It was quite the scene, the most shocking experience of her life, a moment she'd never forget. Camera phones flashed in her face, and she hoped his dramatic, over-the-top proposal wouldn't be posted online for the world to see. "Dante, I can't do this. It's wrong."

"If loving you is wrong I don't want to be right."

"Stop quoting Percy Sledge and listen to me."

"Jordana, baby, I'm all ears. Tell me what's on your mind."

His gaze zeroed in on her, and his deadly sexy smile made a moan catch in her throat, and her sex tingle. *Damn him!* His good humor was contagious, making it impossible for her to stay mad at him. Dante was hard to resist, and if she let her guard down, even for a minute, she'd be putty in his hands. He was a great guy, but marriage was sacred. Not something to joke about. Jordana didn't want to deceive their friends and family, especially her mom. If she did, Helene would never forgive her.

"Do me a favor, would ya? Say yes." He spoke quietly, just loud enough for her to hear, tenderly caressing her fingers with his own. "We have an audience, and if you reject me my brothers will never let me live it down. You don't want me to be the butt of their jokes, do you?"

A giggle escaped her mouth. Jordana was mad at herself for laughing, but she couldn't help it. His sensuous voice, coupled with the scent of his spicy cologne, made it hard for her to think, let alone talk. Dante's charm had the power to transform any situation, and when she remembered their conversation at Griffith Park, her heart softened and her anger abated. This wasn't for show, or a ruse to drum up more business for The Brokerage Group or Morretti Realty. This was a desperate father trying to protect his son. Moved by compassion, she slowly nodded. "Okay, I'll do it."

Dante jumped to his feet, swooped her up in his arms and swung her around the room. The bouquet fell from her hands and tumbled to the ground, sending flowers everywhere.

"She said yes!" he shouted, pumping his fist in the air. "She actually said yes!"

His reaction was endearing and sweet.

"I'm going to kiss you now," he whispered, seizing her in his arms. "Just act natural."

No! Jordana screamed, but the word got trapped inside her throat.

In a blink, she was in his arms, flat against his chest, experiencing the pleasure of his kiss for the first time. He didn't disappoint. He kissed her deeply, thoroughly, with remarkable tenderness. Jordana didn't know what to do, but in typical Morretti fashion, Dante took the reins.

In that moment, nothing else mattered. The world, and everything in it, ceased to exist. Forgetting they had an audience, Jordana gave herself permission to live in the moment, to enjoy being in his arms, and his kiss. She hadn't had sex in nine months, longer if she counted the last time she'd actually had an orgasm. Her body needed this, wanted it.

Dante moved his lips against hers, took his time pleasing her with his tongue. Goose bumps flooded her arms, and zipped along her spine. His caress made her feel alive, and caused her body to throb with desire. He cupped her face in his hands, urging her to come closer. At his touch, her heart jumped for joy. He tasted sweet, like chocolate, and she was hungry for more. *I can't believe it. This is* really *happening. Dante's kissing me and it's perfect. The best kiss I've ever had.*

Desperate to be closer to him, she linked her arms around his neck, swallowing the space between them. Her breathing sped up, and her nipples hardened under her dress, aching to be kissed, caressed and licked. Jordana couldn't stop herself from stroking his face, his shoulders, and burying her hands into his hair. He wanted a show, wanted the world to think they were madly and desperately in love, and Jordana played her role to the T.

Dante pulled away, ending the kiss, and Jordana was overwhelmed with disappointment. It was a surreal moment, one she couldn't wrap her mind around. Her head was spinning so fast she couldn't catch her breath. *Did that just* really *happen?*

"To Jordana!" Dante shouted, hugging her to his side. "Champagne for everyone!"

Chapter 8

An hour after escorting Jordana out of LA Marketing Enterprises and into his Mercedes-Benz SL500, Dante pulled up to his estate on the most prestigious street in Bel Air. Leaning out the window, he punched in his password on the security panel, and waited for the gates to open.

Seconds later, he drove up the cobblestone driveway and past the bronze water fountain. He chanced a look at Jordana. She was staring aimlessly out the window, had been since they entered the car, seemingly lost in her own world. He'd tried talking to her, but every time he asked her a question she had given him a curt, one-word answer.

Troubled by her silence, he tried to read her thoughts by studying her facial expression. Her forehead was creased with wrinkles, and her lips were a hard line. Dante suspected she was angry, felt it rolling off of her in waves. *Is she pissed because I kissed her?* He hoped not, because it was the best kiss he'd ever had, and he needed more. He couldn't stop thinking about her lips, how delicious they tasted, and imagined himself stealing another kiss.

Seeing her frown, he wondered what was on her mind. *Did she enjoy the kiss? Did I come on too strong? Is she going to call off our engagement?* Expelling a deep breath, Dante told himself to relax, to maintain his cool. They had plenty of time to talk, to get everything out in the open, and he was confident by the time he left for his six o'clock business meeting they'd be on the same page. *We better be, because I don't have a plan C.*

"That was some stunt you pulled this afternoon."

Her voice was quiet, lacking its usual warmth and excitement. Maybe things weren't as bad as he thought. Relieved she was finally talking to him, Dante wore an apologetic smile. "I'm sorry. I know the proposal was a bit over-the-top—"

"Ya think?" she quipped, her tone dripping with sarcasm.

"Don't be mad. It was all in good fun."

"I'm not mad, just disappointed. I told you I needed some time."

"I had no choice. I have to act now, before it's too late."

"Is Lourdes still threatening to move to Boston with Matteo?"

Dante gripped the steering wheel so hard his knuckles turned white. Chocked up with emotion and unable to speak, he nodded in response.

"Are you scared of losing him? Is that why you're doing this?"

"Yeah, and I'll do anything to win sole custody, even propose to my sexy actress friend."

He'd hoped his words would earn him a laugh, or at the very least a smile, but Jordana turned away. Instead of talking to him, she fiddled with the bangles on her wrist.

Silence engulfed the car. Dante hated it, but he didn't

know what to say to lighten the mood. His fears of losing Matteo were real, so terrifying he couldn't sleep at night. But since he couldn't articulate his thoughts without sounding like a wuss, he kept his mouth shut. Morretti men were strong, not vulnerable and afraid, and he didn't want Jordana to think less of him. He couldn't open up to her, not about this. After all, their engagement was a sham, not the real deal.

"I didn't know you had a house in Bel Air."

"That's because I just bought it." Dante parked in front of the ten-car garage. "We've only been here a couple of weeks, but it already feels like home, and Matteo loves it."

"I bet. This place is gorgeous."

Dante didn't want to sound conceited, but he had to agree. "You're right, it is."

The Italian-style mansion had more amenities than a five-star hotel. It sat on ten acres of manicured grounds, with towering palm trees providing security and protection, and Dante felt it was the perfect place to raise his son. Over the years he'd sold million-dollar homes to kings, dignitaries and Oscar winners, and knew the moment he saw the estate that it was "the one." And the awestruck expression on Jordana's face proved he'd chosen wisely. The custom-made home, designed by famed architect Warrick Carver, had four master bedrooms, a screening room, heated pool and Jacuzzi, and a basketball court that would make any basketball player jealous.

Dante hopped out of the car, strode around the hood and opened the passenger side door. "I hope you're hungry, because I asked Thierry to prepare a special vegan meal for you. It's waiting in the main-floor dining room."

Her eyes brightened, and her frown morphed into a smile. "You don't even have to ask. You know how I feel about Chef Thierry! He's a culinary genius."

Helping Jordana to her feet, he activated the car alarm and led her up the walkway.

Dante took off his sunglasses, and dropped his keys inside the glass bowl on the side table. The tantalizing aroma wafting out of the kitchen made his mouth wet, and his stomach roar. "We'll eat, then discuss the prenup."

"Prenup?" Jordana shook her head, as if disgusted, and folded her arms across her chest. "You've thought of everything, haven't you, oh Controlling One?"

"Don't get upset. It's nothing—"

"Good, then let's discuss it now. Lunch can wait."

"It can? But I haven't had anything to eat since breakfast, and it's almost two o'clock."

"I'm not going anywhere until we talk." Her mind made up, she marched into the kitchen, pulled out a chair and sat down at the table. Clasping her hands together, she narrowed her eyes. She wore a don't-mess-with-me expression on her face. "I'm waiting."

What's with the attitude? Dante wanted to ask Jordana what her problem was, but something told him not to. It was a miracle that she'd said yes to his proposal, and since he didn't want her to change her mind, he marched into his office, grabbed the contracts off his desk and returned to the kitchen seconds later. "Like I said, it's nothing. I want to be honest and up-front about everything so there are no surprises later."

"As if." Snorting, she swiped the contract from his hand, and flipped to page one. "I don't understand why you even think this is necessary. We're just pretending to be married."

It's all fun and games until someone gets hurt, he thought sadly, blocking out the pain of his past. *I learned my lesson three years ago, and I won't be fooled again.*

"I'd never do anything to hurt you. You know that, right?"

Dante raised an eyebrow. Was Jordana being truthful? Could he trust her? Or would she end up betraying him like his ex-wife? He felt like a fraud for lying, but said, "I know." He didn't. Only time would tell. But to win custody of his son, Dante was willing to roll the dice.

As he watched Jordana review the five-page contract, he considered what she'd said. The divorce had changed him, and not for the better. He used to be a life-of-the-party type who made friends easily. But after his marriage crumbled and Lourdes vilified him in the press, he'd made a conscious decision to keep everyone at arm's length. As much as he respected her, he worried she'd end up using him to advance her acting career, or worse, sell him out to the tabloids. Hence, the need for an iron-clad prenuptial agreement. He'd started Morretti Realty with his own capital, after years of sacrifice and hard work, and he was determined to protect his interests. And his heart. "Once you finish reading the contract you'll see that I've been more than fair."

"When would you like to get married?"

"On Friday."

Her lips parted in surprise, and a gasp fell out. "In three days?

"Yes. We'll get our marriage license at the courthouse, then marry in the judge's chambers."

"A quickie marriage? People will think I'm pregnant."

"Works for me!" Dante chuckled. "The more people talking about us the better."

"How long do we have to stay married for?"

"You make it sound like a prison sentence."

Her eyes darted away from his. To put her at ease, he spoke with confidence, as if he had all the answers. Though, he didn't, and that scared the hell out of him. "I could get custody in a few weeks, or in several months.

But I'm hoping the family court judge makes a decision at our August hearing."

"Dante, are you sure about this? Have you really thought this thing through?"

"Absolutely. I wouldn't be a successful businessman if I didn't. I've weighed all the pros and cons, and determined a marriage of convenience is the smartest course of action."

Hearing his cell phone buzz, he broke off speaking, and retrieved it from his pocket. Dante checked the number on the screen. A scowl curled his lips. *This woman is going to be the death of me!* Lourdes wanted to meet, to discuss their "deal," but Dante wasn't interested, feared he'd lose his temper if they did.

Disgusted, he dropped his cell on the counter, and faced Jordana. Just looking at her made him hard. Astonishingly beautiful, with doe-shaped eyes, high cheekbones and dewy brown skin, it was impossible not to stare at her. "Don't worry. I know what I'm doing."

"Do you? Because I think you're willfully trying to hurt your ex-wife."

Her words didn't surprise him. As expected, she was having doubts. Dante wondered if Jordana was thinking about Tavares. He'd called his buddy last night, to give him a heads-up about the proposal before the media got wind of the story. He ended up leaving a message on his voice mail. "You're wrong. This isn't about her. This is about doing what's best for Matteo." He tried to appear cool, even though his heart was beating at an erratic pace. "Are you worried our fake marriage will ruin your chances of getting back together with Tavares?"

A dark shadow crossed her face. "No, of course not. I've moved on with my life."

"Good, because I don't want you to resent me, or hate me in the future."

Her expression softened, and she spoke in a matter-of-fact voice, as if she was an expert on affairs of the heart. "I know you love Lourdes, and you're still upset about the divorce, but—"

To silence her, he cut her off midsentence. "I don't love her, and I'm not upset about the divorce. It was for the best, and to be honest I prefer being single. Always have."

"Then why are you so mad at her? Why do you hate her with a passion?"

Because she humiliated me, and betrayed my trust. His thoughts returned to the exact moment Ms. Papadopoulos had called. Not being able to help Matteo was the most helpless feeling in the world, one he didn't want to ever experience again. Swallowing hard, he loosened the knot of his Burberry tie to alleviate the pain in his throat. "I won't lose my son."

"Have you tried talking to Lourdes? Surely you guys can work something out."

Hearing his stomach growl, Dante opened the fridge and searched around for a snack. Lunch was waiting in the dining room, but he couldn't eat until Jordana signed the prenuptial agreement. "Can I get you something to drink?"

"No, but you can answer my question."

"You don't know Lourdes. She's a sorry excuse for a mother, and I have zero respect for her. If it were up to me she'd only have supervised visits with Matteo. She doesn't know anything about raising a child."

"What a horrible thing to say!"

No, it's the truth. Dante strode back across the room, and sat down at the table. Setting the water bottle down in front of her, he noted the hostile expression on Jordana's face. He felt her eyes on him, watching him, judging him. Jordana looked pissed, and she stared at him with such contempt he felt ashamed for bad-mouthing his ex.

Guilt troubled his conscience, making him feel lower than a snake. He couldn't think about his marriage without feeling bitter, but he had to do a better job of controlling his emotions. He didn't want Jordana to think he was a sore loser. Her opinion mattered to him, and he wanted to impress her, not turn her off.

Why? questioned his inner voice. *You're friends, not lovers, and that will never change.*

"Lourdes is the mother of your child, and she deserves your respect." Jordana wasn't shouting, didn't raise her voice, but her anger was evident. "She isn't perfect, but no one is. That's what life's about. Making mistakes, learning from them and doing better."

Dante opened his water bottle. "I don't want to argue about this."

"Me neither, but your comments about Lourdes are offensive."

They are? To whom? His ex was calculating and vindictive. If not for Matteo, he'd have nothing to do with her. Tired of talking about Lourdes, and anxious to seal the deal, he reached into his pocket, retrieved his Mont Blanc pen and placed it on the table. "Is there anything else you'd like to discuss before we sign the contracts?"

Dante tasted his drink, watched as fine lines wrinkled her smooth brow.

"What about sex?"

Water spewed out of his mouth, and trickled down his chin. He took the silk handkerchief out of his jacket pocket, and cleaned his face. He could tell Jordana was trying not to laugh—her nose was twitching, and her lips held a smirk. Although he was embarrassed for making a fool of himself, he was glad she'd finally stopped glaring at him. "What about it?"

"Do you expect me to sleep with you?"

Yes, baby, please do! At the thought of sexing Jordana—on his desk, against the pool table, in his Porsche—his temperature soared, and a grin claimed his lips. "Do you want to?"

"Dante, be serious."

I am. Do you have any idea how much I want you? He remembered their kiss, how she'd eagerly responded to his touch, and felt an erection rise inside his boxer briefs. His hands itched to caress her, longed to squeeze and stroke her curves, and images of them rolling around his bed—naked—bombarded his mind.

Afraid of coming on too strong, and scaring her off, Dante broke free of his thoughts and tore his gaze away from her mouth. To keep himself from crossing the line, he pushed his chair away from the table, and buried his wayward hands in his pockets. "I'll expect you to be faithful. You can't date or take lovers if that's what you're asking."

"And you can?"

"No, the same rules apply to me."

Jordana didn't speak, but he sensed she was pleased by the look in her eyes.

"Nothing's going to change, Jordana, except your home address." To reassure her, he smiled good-naturedly. "We'll still be the best of friends, only now we'll be living together."

Jordana pointed at the contract with an index finger, drew his attention to the paragraph on the bottom of page three. "About my weekly allowance..."

"It's not enough? No problem. I'll double it."

"No, don't, it's too much."

"Too much?" Dante repeated,. "Come again?"

"I don't need ten thousand dollars a week. To be honest, I don't need anything. Living here, rent free in this breathtaking estate, is payment enough."

His mouth dropped open. Her words stunned him, and if Dante wasn't already sitting down, he probably would've keeled over on the marble floor. He'd never, ever in all his years heard of anyone repeatedly refusing money. This was a first. But Jordana wasn't just anyone. She was special, unlike anyone he had ever met. Her independent I'm-every-woman attitude was a turn-on.

"And," she continued, "I'm returning the money you put into my account yesterday. I appreciate the gesture, but I don't accept handouts, and I never will."

"Jordana, you're my fiancée now, and if your account's in the red people will talk."

"Which people?"

Dante scoffed. "Nosy-ass bank employees who snitch to the local newspapers."

"Really? No way!"

"These days, everyone's a spy, eager to leak stories to the media for a quick buck. I can't have that. Our marriage has to appear rock solid, especially in the eyes of the court, or I'll never win custody of Matteo."

Jordana wore a sheepish smile. "I didn't even think of that."

"You're keeping the money. End of story. Understood?"

"Are you always this bossy?"

Dante chuckled, and to his relief Jordana did, too.

"Since you're making demands, I have a few of my own."

"Fire away. I'm listening."

Jordana raised her right hand, and stuck out her thumb. "Number one, no more working weekends. Number two, no monthlong overseas business trips. And number three, I expect you home in time for dinner every night."

Dante wore a blank face. Her rules were unrealistic, unreasonable, too, considering he had not one, but two high-paying jobs. But to appease her he nodded in agreement, even promised to cook two nights a week. "You drive a hard bargain, Ms. Sharpe."

"Mr. Lundqvist doesn't call me The Closer for nothing."

With those lips, and that body, your name should be Hot Like Fire, he thought.

"This just might work." Tilting her head to the left, she stared at him through her long, dark eyelashes, a playful expression on her face. "You know this is crazy, right? Engaged today, married on Friday. I'm going to be the talk of the water cooler on Monday—"

"You can't go back to LA Marketing. You have to quit."

Her smile withered like a flower in the hot sun. "Why?"

"Because you're going to be a Morretti, and Morrettis don't work for minimum wage."

"That's ridiculous. I'm my own person, and marrying you isn't going to change that."

"You should be happy. You've been talking about quitting for months."

"You're right, I have, but I don't appreciate you telling me what to do."

Rising from the table, her hands planted on her hips, she spoke in an authoritative voice. Dante liked how she carried herself, and her Lord-have-mercy shape, but it was her eyes that got him. What drew him in every time. Like right now. Jordana was reaming him out, but he didn't defend himself because he was too busy admiring her physical assets. *If not for Tavares, I would've made my move a long time ago.*

"I'm not a puppet, and if you think you can boss me around once we're married you're sadly mistaken because I don't answer to anyone."

Jordana marched off, grumbling about him being a control freak, and Dante had to sprint down the hall to catch up to her. "Jordana, don't go." Worried she'd change her mind, he wore a contrite smile. "Let's talk about this."

To his relief, Jordana stopped. She refused to look at him, kept her eyes on the picture window overlooking the infinity pool, but Dante wasn't fazed. He'd come too far to turn back now, and refused to give up. He stepped forward, got close enough to see the freckles on her nose, and catch a whiff of her lavender perfume. "I'm not trying to control you. I'm thinking about your future. This is your opportunity to better yourself and achieve your lifelong goals."

"School is not for everyone," she argued, dropping her gaze to the mosaic tile floor. "I did two years at Drake University, but it just wasn't for me."

"Who said anything about college? Enroll in acting classes. Take part in local plays and community theater. Get in front of as many casting directors as possible. They'll not only begin to recognize you, but remember you, as well."

"You make it sound so easy. Do you have any idea how many auditions I've been to over the last six years?" Her voice broke, but she spoke through her pain. "How many times I've been told I'm not good enough? Not pretty enough? Not thin enough?"

"It doesn't matter what the haters say. Success is yours for the taking. But you have to fight for it. If this is what you want, don't let anything stand in your way."

Jordana sighed heavily, as if the weight of the world was on her shoulders.

"You're destined to be a star," he said confidently, hoping his words inspired her. "Our marriage could turn out to be the biggest break of your career, so sit back and enjoy the ride."

"I don't like the idea of being a kept woman."

"You're not. You're helping me take care of Matteo, and that's a huge job."

Her eyebrows drew together in a questioning slant. "It is?"

"Absolutely. I could hire a live-in nanny. But I'd rather have you here than someone who knows nothing about me or my son."

"I never looked at it that way."

"You should." Dante slid a hand around her waist. He liked holding her, loved how she felt in his arms, and her soothing scent. "You're the perfect person to play my wife."

"I am? Why?"

"Because you're an incredible woman with a beautiful spirit."

A smile brightened her eyes. "Incredible, huh?"

"Damn right." Dante sniffed the air. "*And* you smell good, too!"

"What will your family think about all this? Won't they be disappointed that you ran off and got married without telling them?"

"They'll understand. They know how much Matteo means to me," he said. "What about you? Are you going to call your parents and tell them the good news?"

"No way. The less they know about our arrangement the better."

Dante stroked his jaw. Her icy tone and the sober expression on her face confused him. *Was Jordana embarrassed by him? Was she afraid her parents wouldn't like him?* He started to speak, but something stopped him from questioning her. It wasn't important. All that mattered was winning custody of Matteo, and keeping him far away from Lourdes. To lighten the mood, he joked, "Do we have a deal, or do I have to post an ad for a temporary wife online?"

"I'll..." She paused, then flashed a smile. "I'll see you at the courthouse on Friday."

"That's my girl!"

"And don't you forget it," she quipped. "You can trust me, Dante. I have your back."

Chapter 9

Jordana didn't see the kiss coming. If she had, she would've turned away before Dante crushed his lips to her mouth. Or at least that's what she told herself as she tried to break free of his grasp. It was a feeble, halfhearted attempt, and when Dante tightened his hold around her waist, she melted into his chest. He smelled good. Felt good. Tasted good. One kiss, and Jordana was hooked. It took everything in her not to push him to the ground, and rip off his clothes.

Lost in the moment, she closed her eyes, and draped her arms around his neck, pulling him close. It was their second kiss of the day—a shocking statistic considering they were friends without benefits. This time Jordana wasn't letting him go until she had her fill. They kissed passionately, fervently, as if their next breath depended on it. His lips were on her mouth, then her ears, her neck and shoulders. His hands got in the mix, too, playing with her curls, caressing her arms, cupping and squeezing her ass.

Rap music shattered the silence, and Jordana snapped to attention, surfacing from her sexual haze. "Dante, stop." Panting her words, she braced her hands against his chest to keep him—and those juicy lips—at bay. "We shouldn't be doing this."

"You're the one who's always telling me to live in the moment and go with the flow," he reminded her. "So, practice what you preach."

His cell phone stopped ringing, but started up again seconds later.

"Do what feels right." Dante moved closer, swallowing the space between them by taking a step forward. "Do you know what feels right to me, Jordana? Making love to you."

His bold declaration, and the sound of his dreamy tone, sent shock waves through her body. Sleeping together would only complicate things, and Jordana didn't want history to repeat itself. She had a horrible track record with men, and wanted to focus on her acting career, not her love life. Women approached Dante at every turn, day in and day out, and he loved the attention. That was reason enough to stick to their arrangement. "Dante, I'm not that kind of girl. I don't do booty calls, or hook up with my friends."

"I'm not asking you to. I'm asking you to revise the terms of our agreement..."

Jordana should have been offended, upset that he was boldly undressing her with his eyes, but she was turned-on, more aroused than she'd ever been. It felt good to be desired, and if not for her disastrous dating history, she'd be all over him. "Dante, I won't be your plaything. I deserve more than that."

"I'm not looking for a relationship. Not right now. I have to focus on Matteo."

"And I have to do what's right for me. How would it look if I slept with you—"

"We're adults, not kids. We don't have to answer to anybody about what we do behind closed doors. Besides, we're engaged. We're supposed to be having amazing sex."

His cell phone vibrated, buzzing incessantly.

"Answer it. It's obvious someone *really* wants to talk to you."

"Sorry. It's Markos," he said, wearing an apologetic smile. "It better be important or I'm going to kick his ass for bothering us."

Jordana laughed, but she was glad for the interruption. She needed a few minutes to gather herself. She sighed in relief when Dante marched over to the table and grabbed his iPhone. *He sure knows how to wear a suit*, she thought, admiring his trim physique.

Dante put the phone to his ear, and shouted into the device. "What?" he growled, his voice colder than ice. "Why are you blowing up my phone?"

Catching sight of her reflection in the bronze mirror hanging beside the cupboard, Jordana fluffed her unruly hair, and straightened her dress.

"When did this happen? Was Matteo with her? Is she in police custody?"

Panicked, Jordana whipped around. She watched as Dante sank into the closest chair, and dropped his face in his hands. To comfort him, Jordana crossed the room, and rested a hand on his forearm. Holding her breath, she waited for Dante to end his phone call, and tell her what was going on.

"I can't say I'm surprised," he said, his tone resigned. "I saw this coming."

Jordana frowned, staring at Dante in confusion. It didn't make sense. His voice sounded grave, as if he'd received horrible, life-changing news, yet he smiled. Jordana wanted to question him but she exercised self-control. Patience had never been her strong suit, and the more time passed, the more her hands sweat, her heart raced and knots coiled inside her stomach.

"Thanks for giving me the heads-up, bro. Tell Officer Núnez I said good work."

Dante ended the call, and placed his cell phone on the table. He didn't say anything, just stared off into space with a pensive expression on his face.

"What's wrong?" Jordana asked, filled with curiosity. "What happened?"

"Lourdes was arrested."

"Arrested? What for?"

"Driving under the influence."

"Are you sure? Maybe it's just a crazy rumor. You know how LA is."

"It's not a crazy rumor," he said sharply. "Markos has a friend in the LAPD who called and informed him of the arrest..."

Her heart ached for Lourdes, and Matteo. To this day, some twenty years later, she still remembered the bitter pain of seeing her mother struggle with substance abuse. Growing up poor, and watching Helene work night and day to make ends meet, Jordana had a great appreciation for single moms. She hoped Lourdes would get the help she needed.

"An officer spotted her driving erratically through her neighborhood, and pulled her over. She failed the Breathalyzer test, then became loud and belligerent with the officer."

"Oh, no, that's awful."

"No, that's karma," he countered.

A thought popped in her mind, chilling her to the bone. "Was Matteo in the car?"

Dante released a deep sigh. "No, thank God. He doesn't have school today, so he's spending the day with Lourdes's younger sister. Chanelle is a pediatric nurse, and she has a couple kids around his age so I know Matteo's in good hands."

"I feel so useless. I wish there was something I could do to help."

"Lourdes got herself in this mess, and she can get herself out of it."

His cell phone rang, and he glanced down at the screen.

"Speak of the devil!" Dante barked a laugh. "Lourdes must be out of her damn mind."

"Why? What is it?"

"She's calling me collect from jail."

"And you're not going to answer it? Why not?"

He gave her an odd look. "Isn't it obvious? She's selfish and inconsiderate, and I want nothing to do with her."

"Dante, she's the mother of your child."

"So? What does that have to do with anything?"

"I think you should bail her out."

"And I think you should spend the night."

His eyes found hers, held her in their seductive grip. But Jordana remained strong, stayed the course. Flirting with Dante would lead to kissing, then touching and undressing. Now more than ever she needed a clear head. "Please reconsider—"

"There's nothing to reconsider." Dante picked up his bottle, downed the rest of his water, and crushed it in his hands. "We're divorced. She's not my problem anymore, and I won't let her pull the wool over my eyes ever again."

"You need Lourdes just as much as she needs you."

"Trust me. I don't." Dante stood. "Make yourself at home. I shouldn't be long."

Jordana jumped to her feet. "Are you going to the police station?"

"No, my office. Markos is going to file for emergency custody on my behalf and I need to fax him the necessary paperwork within the hour."

"If you're getting custody, then you don't need me. We don't have to get married."

"You're wrong. I need you now more than ever."

"I'll marry you, but I need you to do me a favor."

"Sure, Jordana, anything."

"Bail Lourdes out of jail, and pay for her to go to rehab."

His face hardened like stone. "Why?" he asked, through clenched teeth. "Why do you care what happens to my ex-wife?"

"Because, I see myself in Lourdes—"

"That's ridiculous. You're not a raging alcoholic…"

No, but I've made a lot of mistakes and I've done things I'm deeply ashamed of.

"Jordana, stay out of this. It doesn't concern you."

The ferocity of his tone, and the wounded expression on his face, shocked her, making her feel guilty for speaking her mind. Her mom had raised her to stand for what was right, but Jordana feared she'd misspoke. Dante was someone she could always count on, and she was mad at herself for upsetting him. She wanted to tell Dante everything—about her turbulent childhood, her love-hate relationship with her dad, and her wild, reckless college years—but her lips wouldn't form the words. Dante was a perfectionist who'd lived a charmed life, and he wouldn't understand the stupid choices she'd made. "I care about Matteo, and I know how much he loves his mom," she said quietly, wishing he'd quit glaring at her. "To thrive, children need *both* parents, and I'd hate to see him caught in the cross fire in your battle with Lourdes. He's a great kid, and for his sake I want it to stay that way."

"I thought you were an aspiring actress. When did you become a child psychologist?"

Jordana ignored the jab. She had to keep her eye on the big picture, on what mattered most. "For Matteo's sake, extend an olive branch to Lourdes, and work toward being friends."

"Friends? You're kidding me, right?" Dante wore a blank look, staring at her with a disgusted expression on his face. "I believe in moving forward, not backward, so being buddies with my ex-wife is definitely out of the question."

"Please?" she begged, pleading for his understanding. She'd always had a soft spot for single moms, for women who'd fallen on hard times, and felt compelled to advocate for Lourdes. From what she'd seen, Lourdes loved and adored Matteo. Dante couldn't convince her otherwise. "I'll never ask you for anything again. I swear."

His mouth thinned. She could see the emotional roller coaster he was on, and wondered if she'd made a mistake, pushed him too far.

"I'll return the money you put into my bank account. You can use it to bail Lourdes out—"

"Enough." His voice was resigned, tinged with pain. "I'll do it."

"Thanks, Dante. You're doing the right thing—" Jordana broke off speaking. He grabbed his cell phone off the counter, and stormed out of the kitchen. Hearing a door slam, she hung her head, fearing she'd hurt the only man who'd ever given a damn about her.

Chapter 10

"It looks like congratulations are in order."

Dante entered the third-floor conference room at The Brokerage Group head office, and spotted Sergey Smirnov, the company CFO, standing at the head of the table. He gave a polite nod. The Russian businessman had an ego the size of his native country and a penchant for four-letter words. Dante didn't like him, hated the way he bullied his staff. But since he loved his job and wanted to keep it, he smiled and shook his boss's outstretched hand. "Thank you, sir."

"I saw your proposal on the evening news, you sly dog. I didn't even know you were seeing someone, and I make it my business to know *everything* about my employees, especially those in senior management." Mr. Smirnov gave a hearty chuckle. "I look forward to meeting your fiancée. She's stunning, and from what I hear, a talented, up-and-coming actress, as well."

"That she is, but Jordana is more than just a pretty face. She's smart, vivacious and—"

"Fantastic in bed, right? Spanish chicks always are." Mr. Smirnov gave him a shot in the ribs with his elbow. "My third wife is Columbian, and she puts the *F* in freak!"

The six board members seated around the table cracked up, but Dante didn't laugh. Normally, he ignored Mr. Smirnov's off-colored jokes, but not today. "Sir, your comments are offensive and disrespectful."

"Relax, Dante, I'm just busting your chops." Winking, he broke into a broad grin. "Everyone knows Asian chicks are the best lovers. They're nimble as hell!"

Disgusted, Dante glanced discreetly at his gold Breguet wrist watch. He didn't have time to shoot the breeze with Mr. Smirnov; he had to be downtown in ninety minutes. He'd spent the morning meeting architects and engineers about a proposed condo unit in Hollywood, then visited the high-end strip mall complex being built in Santa Monica. He didn't have breakfast, had guzzled down an energy drink as he drove Matteo to school, and didn't have time for dinner. He wanted to see Jordana tonight, but it was impossible. She'd just have to understand. Yesterday, when he'd dropped her home, she'd suggested they take Matteo to Family Arcade for pizza and games. Even though he knew his schedule was jam-packed, he'd readily agreed. He had to, had no choice. He wanted to marry Jordana on Friday, and would do anything to appease her—even if it meant telling a small lie or two. As promised, he'd paid his ex-wife's bail, but held off from writing the check for rehab. Why waste his hard-earned money? Pleased he'd been granted emergency custody, nothing could ruin his good mood. Not even his scheming ex-wife.

"Everyone out. I need to speak to Dante alone."

One by one, Armani-clad board members filed out of the room. Mr. Smirnov stood at the door, smiling, shaking hands, laughing so hard his wiry brown hair tumbled around his head.

Taking a seat at the table, Dante considered his predicament. He'd make it up to Jordana tomorrow. He would find a way to smooth things over before their courthouse wedding. They weren't married yet, so technically he'd done nothing wrong. Furthermore, her request was impossible. Being home every night for dinner wasn't feasible, not with his crazy schedule, and he wasn't going to let Jordana make him feel guilty for working. He had an appointment with city zoning officials at five o'clock, and cancelling it could delay the permit. Without them, construction couldn't start on Dolce Vita Beverly Hills, and the project was already three months behind schedule. He wanted to spend the entire day with Jordana tomorrow, planned to treat her to lunch at her favorite restaurant and a shopping spree on Rodeo Drive. It was imperative he complete everything on his to-do list before calling it a day.

Mr. Smirnov closed the door, strode across the room and plopped down on the side of the table. He smelled of cigar smoke and vodka, and the stench polluted the air.

"Good news," he announced. "Mr. Quan is arriving in LA on Sunday morning…"

His spirits sank.

"Clear your schedule. He's only in town for a few days, so we have to make every second count." Mr. Smirnov nodded to emphasize his point. "Nothing is more important than impressing Mr. Quan, so forget about your curvy new fiancée, and get your head in the game."

Dante was conflicted, unsure of what to do. He didn't want to spend the week wowing Mr. Quan. He wanted to spend it hanging out with Jordana and Matteo at his Bel Air estate. He'd planned to have a dinner party for the Chinese billionaire at the end of the month, not in four days' time. *What if the businessman saw through his marriage charade? Would Mr. Quan take his business elsewhere? Would his boss hold him responsible?* Troubling thoughts bombarded his mind, and Dante felt his throat close up. *If the truth gets out will I lose custody?*

"Let's give him the royal treatment," he advised. "Champagne, caviar and strippers go a long way in closing deals."

"Not this time. Mr. Quan is a devout Christian, and I don't want to offend him."

Mr. Smirnov snorted like a potbellied pig, and gave a dismissive wave of his hands. "Devout Christian, my ass. One night at Cheetahs and he'll be singing another tune. Just watch."

"I don't think so. Mr. Quan comes to LA regularly, but he doesn't attend movie premieres or celebrity parties. He loves gospel music, and attends concerts, services and prayer rallies at First AME Church whenever he's in town."

Mr. Smirnov stroked his beard. "I don't have to tell you what this deal could mean to this company, do I?"

"No, sir, you don't." To project confidence, Dante straightened in his chair, and pinned his shoulders back. "I'm well aware of how important it is, and I want you to know that I'm a hundred percent committed to our global expansion plans."

"Good. That's what I wanted to hear." Mr. Smirnov swiped his cell phone off the table, slid his finger across the screen and typed for several seconds. He kept his head glued to his iPhone, but continued speaking. "Now isn't the time to rest on your laurels. Be aggressive. Take risks. Do whatever it takes, you hear me? Whatever. It. Takes."

Dante didn't like Mr. Smirnov's tone, didn't appreciate his boss talking to him as if he was a newbie desperate to make a name for himself in the real estate field. He had a successful track record and business contacts all over the world. He didn't need, nor want, Mr. Smirnov's advice. He'd do the deal his way, or not at all. "I want this contract, but not at the expense of my pride. There are numerous investment opportunities right here in the United States, and I have several lucrative business deals in the works," he explained.

"Yes, but none of them are worth five point two billion dollars."

Anger burned inside him, but he masked his true emotions.

"This deal could make or break us."

"I disagree. To achieve success in the Asian market, we need to diversify, not pin all our hopes and dreams on this one deal. It's imperative we build our reputation, attract international attention and partner with established investment firms known worldwide. If we don't, our five-year global expansion plan will fail miserably."

His smile was as cheap as plastic, but he spoke in a jovial tone. "Well said, Morretti. I agree wholeheartedly." Mr. Smirnov put down his cell phone, and folded his arms across his flabby chest. "I need to discuss something important with you."

"Sure, sir, what's on your mind?"

"I understand that your firm, Morretti Realty & Investments, is working with Ryder Knoxx."

Dante didn't respond, remaining calm and stoic on the outside.

"He wants to buy an estate in Beverly Hills, just miles away from my daughter's home. I can't let that happen. They were married for nine years, and he made her life a living hell."

"I'm sorry to hear that, sir, but your family drama has nothing to do with my company." Dante wore a sympathetic smile, to assure his boss he wasn't choosing sides, but he suspected Mr. Smirnov was feeding him a lie. He'd met the aging rocker several times and found him to be polite, soft-spoken and courteous. “Mr. Knoxx is a client, and I won’t discuss his private affairs with you.”

“Screw him,” he growled, baring his coffee-stained teeth. “He’s a punk who abuses women, and one day I’m going to give him a taste of his own medicine.”

“Sir, with all due respect, I won’t discuss my company, my clients or my personal investments with you.” He pushed back his chair, stood and buttoned his suit jacket. “Now, if you’ll excuse me, I have work to do.”

“Veto the deal.”

Convinced he’d misheard his boss, he stopped and turned around. “Come again?”

“You heard me.” His tone was quiet, but deadly. If his eyebrows were any higher they’d be touching his receding hairline. “I don’t want that creep anywhere near my daughter, so veto the deal, and do it now.”

“And if I don’t?”

Mr. Smirnov flinched, as if he’d been pimp-slapped, but quickly recovered, flashing a smug, superior smile. “I’m not asking you, Dante, I’m telling you.”

“I think you forgot how I came to work for this company, so let me jog your memory. You sought me out,” he said, jabbing a finger at his chest. “I told you I had my own business, but you practically begged me to take this job.”

His face was as red as his burgundy tie. “I didn’t beg you to do shit, Morretti.”

“I’m going to pretend this conversation didn’t happen, and I suggest you do the same.”

Yanking open the door, Dante stalked out of the conference room without another word.

Dante dragged his weary body into the master bedroom of the penthouse suite at W Hollywood, and dumped his briefcase on the reading chair. The black-and-red color scheme was simple, but striking, and the combination of wood, granite and marble created a luxurious feel inside the suite. Leather couches, glass sculptures and dramatic artwork beautified the space.

Yawning, he collapsed onto the platform bed and closed his eyes. He stayed at the hotel whenever he was too tired to drive to Bel Air, or if he had female company. Club-hopping and one-night stands were in the past. Dante wanted his marriage scheme to work, and planned to spend his free time with Jordana and Matteo, not at the local bar or lounge.

Dante sniffed the air. It held the faint scent of Sancho Panza cigars—his favorite vice—and the aroma made him hanker for a smoke. Too tired to move, he unbuttoned his jacket, and loosened the knot on his pin-striped tie. Dante lay there, sprawled out in his Hugo Boss suit, staring up at the ceiling, reviewing his day. His conversation with his boss played in his mind, angering him afresh. Mr. Smirnov had some nerve. If he thought he could control him he was wrong. Dante didn't need The Brokerage Group; they needed him. On the upside, his meeting with city zoning officials had gone well, and construction could start on Dolce Vita Beverly Hills next week. From his Porsche, he'd called his cousin Nicco to share the good news. As with all of his projects, he wanted the restaurant to be completed on time, and under budget. He hoped the establishment would be as successful as the others.

His cell phone rang, filling the silence with rap music. What the hell? Who in their right mind would be calling him after midnight? Dante listened, recognized the "California Love" ringtone and bolted upright in bed. It was Tavares. They'd been boys since college, and Dante missed having him around. Anxious to speak to his friend, he fished his cell out of his pocket, and put it to his ear. "It's about time you hit me back. I've been calling you the last few days with no luck. What's the deal?"

"I was in Abu Dhabi on business, and returned late last night."

"No worries. How's Melbourne? Still thinking about renewing your work visa—"

"When were you going to tell me you and Jordana were an item?"

His mouth dried, but he forced his lips to move. "It's not what you think."

"Good, because for a minute I thought you broke the Bro Code."

"The Bro Code doesn't apply to Jordana," Dante said, prepared to argue his case. "You dumped her, so technically I haven't broken any rules."

"That's beside the point. Man, what's going on? I thought we were boys."

Dante dragged a hand across his neck, massaging his tired, aching muscles. "We are."

"Then why did you propose to my ex-girlfriend?"

"Because Matteo needs a mother."

"Did Lourdes die?"

Dante aired his frustrations, vented to Tavares about his problems with Lourdes. But instead of feeling better, he felt worse. His ex-wife had called him as he was leaving the office, and wasted twenty minutes of his time rambling about her "unauthorized arrest." At the end of her nonsensical rant she'd had the nerve to ask him for a loan. To gain his sympathy, she'd turned on the water works, cried so hard she couldn't speak. But Dante didn't buy her woe-is-me act. It took everything in him not to curse her out for driving drunk in the first place. Remembering his promise to Jordana to keep the peace, he told Lourdes he'd think about, and hung up the phone. *The things I have to do for my son*, he thought, kicking off his leather, Kenneth Cole shoes. *If I get my way, Matteo won't see Lourdes again until she's clean and sober.*

"Let me get this straight. The proposal was just a ploy to win custody of Matteo?"

Dante heard the question, but he didn't answer.

"Are you sure you're not romantically interested in Jordana?"

"What kind of question is that?"

"Just curious. Every time we hung out, you two were always off in a corner, talking and laughing, and I felt like the third wheel. It was obvious Jordana liked you..."

It was? She *does*? Dante loved a woman with an opinion, and Jordana had many. Unlike the females he'd dated in the past, she wasn't afraid to disagree with him and argued her ideas with the confidence of a Supreme Court judge. They had great discussions about hot-button issues, made each other laugh, and her one-liners were a turn-on. "Nothing's going on, man. We're friends."

"What a relief." Tavares released an audible sigh. "Jordana's a good woman who doesn't care about my wealth or status, but I was too full of myself to realize it."

"It sounds like you miss her."

"You have no idea."

"I told you she was a keeper, but you wouldn't listen."

"I know. Don't remind me. Do you think if I call and apologize she'll forgive me?"

Dante shrugged. "I...I...don't know."

"Find out for me. I want to see her the next time I'm in LA."

The silence was profound, as deafening as the music at a rock concert, but Dante couldn't think of anything to say to fill the void.

"I thought Jordana's ninety-day rule was a clever ploy to control me, so I pushed her away and ran around with other girls, but—"

"Hold up. Rewind. *What* ninety-day rule?"

Tavares gave a bitter laugh. "Jordana read this relationship advice book, adopted the rules and gave me hell whenever I messed up."

"But, you guys dated for almost a year."

"I know, but she *still* wouldn't give up that ass. I bought her jewelry, flowers, the works. And she wouldn't take things to the next level."

Dante wanted to hear more, and pushed Tavares for answers. "Why not?"

"I don't know. To be honest, I never felt like I mattered to her. When she refused to join me in Paris for the holidays, and went to whack-ass Des Moines instead, I dumped her."

"Do you want her back?"

"Heck yeah! Haven't you been listening?"

His cell beeped, signaling he had another call coming in. A glance at his phone confirmed it. Lourdes was on the line. Dante pressed Ignore, and returned to the conversation.

"Hey, did you see the Royals game last night?" he asked, anxious to change the subject. "Demetri caught fire in the ninth inning, and the Sharks couldn't do anything to stop him…"

They talked about baseball, their upcoming guys-only trip to Tampa for the RaShawn Bishop Charity Golf Tournament, and their respective careers. Tavares was a systems analyst for a Melbourne-based software company and had dreams of starting his own business. He was wise and perceptive, and Dante decided to open up to him about his day from hell. Dante was recounting his conversation with Mr. Smirnov that afternoon when Tavares interrupted him midword, bombarding him once again with questions about the marriage scheme.

"How long is your fake marriage to Jordana supposed to last?"

Dante scowled. *Why did Tavares have to make it sound so devious?*

"I'm not sure. Three months, maybe less. Once I'm awarded full custody we'll get our marriage annulled, and go our separate ways. Why?"

"I just want to know how long I have to wait to have another crack at her!"

Tavares laughed, and said he was only joking. But Dante didn't believe him.

"I should kick your ass for dragging her into your family drama. She's fragile, you know."

At a loss for words, he stared down at the phone. He'd never use the word *fragile* to describe Jordana. There was nothing weak about her. Tough and feisty, she was determined to make a name for herself in Hollywood, despite the numerous setbacks she'd faced over the years. He suspected it was just a matter of time before Jordana got her big break.

"Jordana's the one I let get away," he confessed. "We broke up months ago, but my parents still ask about her, especially my mom. I think she loves Jordana more than my sister!"

"How's Nadine doing? It's been ages since I saw her. The boys must be big now—"

"That's it! Why didn't I think of it sooner? I know what you should do."

Tavares was shouting so loud Dante had to move his cell phone away from his ear.

"Man, calm down, I'm not trying to go deaf."

"Marry my sister. She'll say yes in a heartbeat."

Dante choked on his tongue. *As if! I wouldn't marry her if you put a gun to my head!*

"Nadine's single."

Of course she was, she was a drama queen who only dates bad boys. The mother of three had a criminal record and zero ambition. Sure, she was easy on the eyes—tall, stacked and voluptuous—but she wasn't his type and they had nothing in common. "Good looking out man, but I need someone with a flexible schedule to help out with Matteo, and your sister already has her hands full with your nephews."

"Fine," he snapped. "Then find someone else, just don't marry my ex."

Taken aback by his anger, Dante didn't realize Tavares had hung up the phone until it went dead. Second thoughts weighed heavily on his mind. Was he making a mistake? Should he marry someone else? Someone he wasn't ridiculously attracted to? The problem was he didn't want anyone else. Only Jordana would do. He knew a lot about her—she loved chai tea and French films, had a wicked sense of humor and was addicted to hot yoga. Dante liked the idea of them living under the same roof. He had to stick to the plan. He'd marry Jordana on Friday, prove to family court why he should have full custody and move on with his life. It was as simple as that, and he wouldn't let anyone—not even his friend—stop him from achieving his goal.

Chapter 11

"Are you nervous?"

Are diamonds a girl's best friend? Of course I'm nervous. Scared out of my mind, actually. I'm deceiving the people I love, and I can't shake the feeling that I'm making the biggest mistake of my life. Unable to control her quivering hands and legs, Jordana paused on the courthouse steps, and took a moment to gather herself. It was barely 9:00 a.m. on Friday morning, but the LA County Courthouse on Ocean Avenue was a hub of noise and activity. Taxicabs were parked at the curb, loading and unloading passengers, businessmen clutched cell phones and coffee cups while trading jokes and laughs, and steely-eyed security guards patrolled the area on foot. "Me? Nervous? No way…" Her throat went dry, and her voice cracked. "Okay, I'm lying. Maybe a little."

"Don't be." Waverly lobbed an arm around Jordana's shoulder and gave her a hug. "You look adorable, and you're having a killer hair day, too. Enjoy it!"

Jordana wrinkled her nose, feeling a bitter taste fill her mouth. *Adorable? I wasn't going for adorable. I was going for sophisticated and sexy!*

"That's her," said a male voice. "I'd recognize that hair and that ass anywhere..."

Turning, she noticed two suits gawking at her, and shot them a dirty look. Video footage of Dante's surprise proposal had gone viral. These days Jordana couldn't go anywhere without being recognized. Men flirted with her, showered her with compliments and begged for her cell number. Worse, her friends and former coworkers were blowing up her phone. They called to congratulate her, and were desperate for the inside scoop on her new millionaire fiancé. Each lie that fell from her mouth intensified Jordana's guilt.

Jordana glanced at her dainty silver watch. In less than an hour she'd be a married woman. Dante's wife. At the thought, goose bumps pricked her skin. Jordana considered calling her mom to give her the heads-up. It was the right thing to do, but she banished the thought. She knew if she did, Helene would be on the first flight to LA, and that was last thing Jordana wanted. Besides, news of their courthouse wedding would never reach Des Moines. Helene didn't own a computer, and rarely watched TV or read the newspaper. But to be on the safe side she'd give her a ring after the ceremony to make sure her secret was still safe. Jordana was looking forward to talking to her mom. Using the money Dante had given her, she'd paid off Helene's debts,. Her mother had questioned her about where the money came from but she'd swiftly changed the subject. She'd also registered for acting classes at Theatre of Arts, and come Monday she'd be a student at the premier acting studio. Thanks to Dante, things were looking up and she was feeling more hopeful about her future.

Her gaze fell across her left hand, and zeroed in on

her engagement ring. It shimmered in the sunlight. Dante didn't just know how to close million-dollar deals, he also knew how to select beautiful jewelry. Jordana couldn't stop staring at it. It was stunning, and having it on her left hand made her feel special, like a somebody.

Whoa, Nelly! yelled her inner voice. *Slow. Your. Roll. You're playing Dante's wife, not* actually *his wife. Don't get caught up in the moment.*

Sunshine splashed through the lobby windows, conversation and laughter filled the space, and the earthy, refreshing scent in the air made Jordana think of the ocean. Last week, she'd gone to Zuma Beach with Dante and Matteo, and remembering how much fun they'd had flying kites and building sand castles made her fears dissipate. *I can do this. I will do this. Marrying Dante could turn out to be the biggest break of my career, and I won't mess this up.*

Boarding the elevator, Jordana checked her reflection in the wall mirror. Her diamond headband made her eyes twinkle, the lace belt on her vintage gown drew attention to her slim waist, and the frilly bow on her sandals made Jordana feel feminine. Busy fussing with her curls, she didn't notice the elevator had stopped until Waverly grabbed her forearm, and dragged her onto the second floor.

"Let's go," she trilled. "We don't want to keep the groom waiting."

Linking arms, the women followed the signs until they arrived at the office of the justice of the peace. Entering the waiting area, Jordana was shocked to see dozens of couples kissing, cuddling and holding hands. Love was in the air, and she smiled as she watched the starry-eyed lovers dote on each other.

"Lookie, lookie, your man's already here. He must be *really* anxious to marry you..."

Jordana rested a hand on her chest, to steady her raging pulse, but it didn't help. Her pulse drummed so loud she couldn't hear what Waverly was saying. Dante was standing beside the water cooler, talking and laughing with his brother. Markos was lean, built like a quarterback, and fine as sin. Everything about him, from his dimpled chin to his full lips and staggering six-foot-six height, was enticing, but Dante was the one who made her heart swoon. Well-groomed, he looked debonair in a crisp white suit. Jordana couldn't take her eyes off him.

What else is new? said her inner voice. *You've had the hots for him ever since you met.*

Watching him aroused her. Delicious sensations flooded her body. Jordana could tell by Dante's jovial disposition that he was in a good mood. Was he excited about the ceremony, or his newest development deal? Jordana told herself it was the latter, had to be. After all, this was a publicity stunt, not a whirlwind love affair. She'd be a fool to think otherwise. "Waverly, knock it off. Dante's not my man and you know it."

"Not yet," she said in an airy voice. "But it's just a matter of time before you're madly in love. You guys are destined to be together."

"You need to stop watching reality TV," Jordana joked. She was nervous enough, battling a serious case of doubts, and the more Waverly teased her about Dante, the queasier her stomach felt. "This is a business deal, and nothing more."

"You'll be lovers by the end of the week."

"Right, and those are your real boobs."

Waverly stuck out her tongue, and patted her chest. "Damn right they are! I paid top dollar for these babies. My only regret is not going bigger!"

The women dissolved into girlish laughter.

"We're friends," Jordana said, composing herself. "Why don't you believe me?"

"Because I see the way he looks at you, and more important, the way *you* look at him," Waverly shot back, poking her hard in the shoulder. "You want him bad. Just admit it."

"Dante's like a brother to me."

"Girl, stop, you're not fooling anyone with that platonic-friends crap, so drop the act. Dante's hot and successful and über-rich. If I were you I'd turn this fake marriage into the real thing because that Italian stallion is every woman's dream."

Dante glanced at his watch, then at the door, and spotted them. His eyes lit up, and he broke into a broad smile. Walking toward her, his face bathed in excitement, he spoke in a strong voice. "Baby, you made it!"

"Of course I did. We have a deal, and I'd never bail on you."

"You're a true friend." Looking her over from head to toe, he added, "And a gorgeous one, as well. This dress was made for you. You have the word *star* written all over you."

His words gave her a rush. While in Des Moines last month running errands for her mom, she'd spotted the silk fit-and-flare gown in a store window and instantly fell in love. Her pearl accessories gave the dress a touch of pizzazz. When Dante took her in his arms and hugged her tight, Jordana knew she'd chosen wisely.

His hands slid across her shoulders, down her hips, lingering on the small of her back. Jordana's mouth dried, and heat crept over her cheeks. His touch was warm, as welcome as an ice-cold drink on a summer day. She felt sexy, desirable and hot. Jordana moaned inwardly, felt another one rising up her throat and bit down hard on her bottom lip to stop it from escaping her mouth. His cologne overwhelmed her senses, stirring strong feelings inside her. Desire. Lust. Need. The urge to kiss him was powerful, all she could think about, but Jordana remembered they had an audience and pulled away.

"It's great to see you again, Jordana. It's been too long." Markos lowered his head, kissed her on each cheek, then whispered in her ear. "I hope you're being adequately compensated for this trip to the courthouse because you're the most beautiful bride in the room."

Flustered by his words, she couldn't speak. "Ah, thanks, Markos. You, too."

He chuckled. The sound of his loud, booming voice made Jordana laugh, too. It was hard to think around Dante and Markos, impossible to keep it together in the presence of such hot, drop-dead sexy men, but she was determined to maintain her composure. "So much for being in and out. Look at all of these people. At this rate, we'll still be here until lunch." Jordana gestured to the ticket dispenser in front of the door. "Did you already grab a number?"

"There's no need. We're next."

"No way. We just got here."

Dante clasped her hand, and gave it a soft squeeze. His touch instantly calmed her nerves. "Judge Abdallah was Markos's law school mentor, and when Markos told him we were madly in love and anxious to get married, he agreed to perform the ceremony first thing this morning."

Waverly looked impressed, and gazed longingly at Markos. "I have a few speeding tickets," she confessed, a sheepish expression on her oval face. "Can you work your magic in traffic court, and make them disappear?"

The men laughed, and Jordana decided then they were the sexiest brothers alive.

"Dante Morretti, Jordana Sharpe and witnesses!" The clerk, a petite redhead in an ill-fitted gray pantsuit, waved them over to her desk. She asked to see two pieces of ID, and helped them fill out the marriage-license application. Ten minutes later, she led them down the corridor and into the office at the end of the hall. It had canary walls, oversize windows that offered Instagram-worthy views of the city. The glass shelves were filled with antiques and collectibles. It was nicely decorated and smelled like a florist shop. But the office was so cramped, Jordana felt as if she was standing inside a broom closet.

"Dante, this is it? This is where we're getting married?"

"What were you expecting?" a male voice asked. "The Four Seasons grand ballroom?"

A short black man, dressed in traditional African clothes, breezed into the room, clutching a Holy Bible in one hand and rosary beads in the other. "It's a great day to get married, so let's do this," he said, pumping his fist in the air. "Any questions? No? Good, because time is money and I'm saving up for a private jet!"

Tossing his head back, he laughed heartily at his own joke.

"He's a judge?" Jordana whispered, dumbfounded. "Are you sure?"

"Positive. Judge Abdallah married my aunt and uncle eleven years ago in Orange County, and to this day we still crack up about the ceremony. He's great. You'll see."

If you say so, she thought, watching the eccentric judge with growing interest.

He took his place in front of the desk, beckoned them over and flipped open the Bible. He didn't read from it, but he sounded official, as if he knew what he was doing. "We are gathered here today to join Dante and Jordana in holy matrimony. You are here of your own free will, and your intention is to marry each other, right?"

Bewildered by the question, Jordana slowly nodded.

"Whew, what a relief," he said, mopping imaginary sweat from his wrinkled brow. "Because I paid an arm and a leg for parking and it's too late to get a refund!"

Jordana noticed the amused expression on Markos's face, saw the corner of his lips twitch, and knew the attorney was trying not to laugh. Judge Abdallah cracked jokes, doled out marriage advice and spoke candidly about his thirty-year marriage. "Dante, don't let anyone come between you and Jordana. She comes first, you hear me, son? Treat her like a queen and she'll reward you with respect, compassion and good lovin'!"

Waverly erupted in laughter, Markos cheered and Jordana choked on her tongue. Dante, to her surprise, seemed to be listening to every outrageous word. He looked relaxed, as if he was enjoying the ceremony. He nodded as Judge Abdallah admonished him to be a loyal, supportive husband. "Son, turn to your bride, and share your vows…"

Facing her, a reassuring smile on his lips, he took her hands in his, and held them tight. "I, Dante, take you, Jordana, to be my lawfully wedded wife. I promise to love you, and protect you, from this day forward, for the rest of my life, as long as we both shall live."

Eyes wide, Jordana heard a gasp escape her lips. Her legs wobbled, banging violently together. Afraid they wouldn't support her weight and she'd fall flat on her ass, she clutched Dante's hands, and dug her heels into the carpet. The L-word scared the hell out of her, dredged up painful memories she wished she could forget, but Jordana loved hearing the word come out of Dante's mouth. Sounding earnest and sincere, he spoke about his hopes for their future. He was one hell of an actor, so damn convincing she almost believed him.

"Well done." Patting Dante on the shoulder, Judge Abdallah nodded in approval. "Your turn, pretty lady. Don't be shy. Tell Dante how you truly feel."

It was hard enough to breathe, let alone think, so Jordana repeated his short, heartfelt speech. Her voice sounded foreign to her ears, as if it belonged to someone else. But she conquered her nerves and spoke with confidence. "I love you, Dante. This is my solemn vow."

"Good job, baby. I couldn't have said it better myself."

Everyone laughed.

As the ceremony went on, her legs quit shaking and her fears disappeared. Judge Abdallah's larger-than-life personality put Jordana at ease and soon she was laughing at his jokes, too. They exchanged rings, then signed the marriage license they'd obtained that morning.

"I now pronounce you man and wife! Now, for the moment we've *all* been waiting for!" Judge Abdallah reached into his pocket, pulled out a handful of red rose petals and tossed them in the air. "You may now kiss your bride. Put it to her good, son. You're a Morretti!"

Jordana closed her eyes, and waited anxiously for his kiss. His kisses were thrilling, second to none, and just the thought of it made her panties wet. Instinctively, her lips parted, and she moved toward him. Dante pressed his mouth to her lips, for all of two seconds, then abruptly pulled away. What the hell? He called *that* a kiss? Though disappointed and confused, she faked a smile, and took the hand he offered.

They took pictures with Judge Abdallah, and left the courthouse with Markos and Waverly in tow. Outside, Jordana felt the sun on her face, the breeze in her hair, and a delectable aroma wafting out of the bakery on West Olympic Boulevard. Strolling down the street, she chatted with her friends about the ceremony, the eccentric judge and where to have lunch.

Fifteen minutes after leaving the courthouse, they entered the JW Marriott, scored a window table inside Ford's Filling Station, and ordered a bottle of Cristal. Taking in her surroundings, Jordana noticed every woman in the room—even married ones sporting massive diamond rings—make eyes at Dante and Markos. Of course they were. What else was new? The brothers couldn't go anywhere without females ogling them like pieces of meat, but they either didn't care or didn't notice because they paid their admirers no mind.

Openly watching Dante, a smile brightened her heart, and claimed her mouth. *Mercy!* Feeling her cheeks warm, she tore her gaze away from his lips, and chose to admire his broad shoulders and trim physique instead. *Damn, he sure knows how to rock a suit! Yum, yum!*

Jordana broke free of her thoughts, but her mind continued to race, spinning faster than the decorative ceiling fan hanging above their booth. An hour after the ceremony, she still couldn't believe she was Mrs. Dante Morretti. If her eyes weren't open, and her mouth wasn't filled with garlic-flavored biscotti, Jordana would swear she was dreaming.

"I love it here. The service is outstanding, and the food is always on point." Picking up a menu, Markos hungrily licked his lips. "I can almost taste the baby back ribs now!"

Jordana admired the chic, contemporary decor. Praised for its California flair, the restaurant was known for its creative menu, five-star service and relaxing ambience. Within seconds of being seated, the waitress arrived with the champagne, and took their orders. "I'll be back shortly with your appetizers."

To pass the time, Markos entertained the group with stories about his law firm. Jordana liked him, thought he had a winning personality, but she didn't want to hear about his celebrity clients or his meteoric rise to judicial fame. She wanted to know what was up with Dante.

Sipping her mineral water, Jordana found herself analyzing their last kiss. *Where was the heat? The passion?* She couldn't make sense of it. Three days ago, he'd wanted to make love to her inside his Bel Air kitchen, and now he was distant. One minute he was hot, the next lukewarm, leaving her feeling lost and confused.

Not to mention sexually frustrated, quipped her inner voice. *You want Dante so bad you can't think straight, and if you don't pull yourself together everyone's going to know the truth.*

Two servers arrived, carrying trays topped with appetizers and entrées, and placed them on the table. "Enjoy. If you need anything just let us know," the waitress said.

Jordana plucked a risotto ball off the plate, and popped it into her mouth. It was flavorful and moist, and she savored every bite. Too nervous to eat, she'd skipped breakfast that morning, and now she was so hungry she wanted to devour everything in sight.

"I'd like to make a toast," Markos announced, reaching for the bottle of champagne.

To prevent him from filling her flute, Jordana covered it with her hands. "None for me."

Dante said, "I know you don't usually drink, but it's a special occasion."

"Tell that to my ass, because that's *exactly* where those extra calories will go!"

"Don't be ridiculous. You're perfect, and you know it."

"You're right," she quipped, fervently nodding her head. "I am!"

Markos cleared his voice, and raised his glass high in the air. "To Dante and Jordana. May your marriage be filled with laughter, happiness *and* hot summer nights!"

Dante cracked up, and Jordana wondered why he was laughing so hard. Their marriage was a sham, sure, but their connection was real, and every time they kissed she melted into his arms. She felt fortunate to be his wife—even if it was just for a few months. Jordana was looking forward to spending the summer with her two favorite boys.

Over lunch, the group chatted about movies, pop culture and their plans for the weekend. Jordana was surprised to hear Dante tell Markos he had to work on Saturday, and made a mental note to remind him about the terms of their prenuptial agreement. He'd made a promise to her, and she was going to ensure he kept his word. Consumed with thoughts of their "marriage," she missed the question posed by Markos, and laughed out loud when he repeated it.

"It's your turn, Jordana. Tell us the worst date you've ever been on."

Groaning, she hung her head at the memory of her first and last blind date. "That's easy. Several years ago my former boss set me up with her younger brother, and midway through dinner he told me he was wearing an ankle bracelet and had to be home by nine."

"No way," Waverly said, cupping a hand to her mouth. "You're lying!"

"That's not all. He stiffed me with the check, and had the nerve to complain to his sister because I refused to go out with him again."

Everyone laughed, except Dante. Wearing a sympathetic smile, he took her hand, raised it to his mouth and kissed it. His touch left her wanting more, and his piercing gaze left her weak. Charismatic, and charming, he knew just what to say to make her feel special.

"Don't give that jerk another thought..."

You don't have to tell me twice! He's so irrelevant I don't even remember his name.

"That's all behind you," he continued. "You have me now, and I'm not going anywhere."

Their eyes lined up, and Jordana swallowed a moan. Her emotions spun out of control, stealing her ability to think, and leaving her speechless. His words played in her ear, like a love song, tingling and teasing her sex. If Markos and Waverly weren't sitting at the table, there was no doubt in her mind that she would have kissed him—a few times.

"Well, it's been fun folks, but I'm out. I'm due in court at four o'clock. If I don't meet with my client beforehand all hell could break loose in the judge's chambers."

"Markos, can you give me a lift to the train station? I'd walk, but I'm beat."

"I'll do you one better. I'll drive you home."

Cheering, Waverly grabbed her purse, and jumped to her feet. "Now, *that's* what I'm talking about. I love exotic sports cars!"

"Then today is your lucky day, because I drove the Lambo." Chuckling, Markos opened his wallet, took out several hundred-dollar bills and shoved them under the empty bread basket. "Lunch is on me. Make sure you guys order dessert. It's your wedding day. Live a little."

After a round of hugs and kisses, Markos and Waverly left the dining area. Alone now, Jordana decided it was the perfect time to talk to Dante about his plans for the weekend. "I'd love to go camping, and so would Matteo. He wants to learn how to fish, and Reflection Lake is filled with salmon, trout, bass, you name it."

"I can't. I'm working at Morretti Realty on Saturday, and on Sunday we're hosting a dinner party at the estate for Chinese billionaire Lu Quan."

"We are?" she questioned, raising an eyebrow. "When were you planning to tell me about your little soiree? The morning *of* the party?"

"My bad. You're right. I should have told you sooner, but with everything going on with work, Lourdes and filing for emergency custody, it slipped my mind."

"Fine, we'll go camping on Memorial Day."

"I'll get back to you," he said, with a shrug. "I have to check my schedule first."

"No, we agreed you wouldn't work weekends. That's family time, remember?"

"I'm the face of Morretti Realty, and it's important I connect with clients—"

Jordana cut him off midsentence, refusing to listen to another lame-ass excuse. "Then we're going to have a problem because we signed a contract and I expect you to honor it."

"I have a lot on my plate, but once I close this deal with Lu Quan, I'm all yours."

"I don't understand why you have two jobs," she said, speaking her thoughts aloud. "It's not like you need the money. You were born with a silver spoon in your mouth, and your family owns everything from restaurants to strip malls and commercial and residential properties."

"Because I love what I do and I'd be bored out of my mind if I wasn't crazy busy."

"Bored out of your mind? That's impossible. You have a four-year-old son who adores you, and he'd be over the moon if you spent more time with him."

"I'll scale back my hours next month so we can take advantage of the nice weather."

"Good idea." Jordana added, "Better yet, quit one of your jobs."

Dante pointed a finger at his chest. "And you say I'm bossy? Ha!"

The waitress arrived, collected the empty plates and thanked them for the generous tip.

"We should go. We have a full day ahead of us."

"We do?" Jordana made her eyes wide. "I thought you were going to the office."

"On my wedding day? No way. I'm playing hooky with my stunning bride, and no one's going to stop me." Grinning like a Cheshire cat, he leaned into her, took her hand in his and intertwined their fingers. "Is that okay with you, Mrs. Morretti?"

Are you serious? Of course it is! she thought, *I can't think of anything I'd like more—except maybe another kiss.* Her pulse throbbed in her ears, making it impossible to think, but she composed herself and spoke in an easy-breezy voice. "Sounds good, Dante. What's on the agenda?"

"To start, a fashionable new wardrobe for you."

"Why? I love my style. It's eclectic, unique and totally me."

His gaze slid down her curves, warming her body all over, from her ears to her toes.

"You're right," he said, with an appreciative nod. "You look great in everything—"

"Then why are you trying to change me?"

"I have an image to uphold, and now that we're married so do you."

Jordana dropped his hand, and folded her arms. "What does *that* mean?"

"That means no more shopping at thrift stores and garage sales," he explained, speaking in a stern voice. "And no more hanging out in the inner city after dark, either. If Waverly wants to see you she can come to Bel Air."

"Anything else, oh Controlling One?"

"You're getting a new car, as well."

"Why? There's nothing wrong with my Mini Cooper."

A scowl darkened his face. "There's duct tape on the bumper. That's unacceptable."

"It gets me from point A to point B and that's all that matters."

"Not when you're a Morretti. Only the best will do."

Jordana was frustrated that Dante was bossing her around again, but she didn't argue. In her family, she was seen as a troublemaker because she didn't do as she was told. Although she prided herself on being a strong, independent woman who didn't need a man, she didn't want to butt heads with Dante every time he did something nice for her. Determined to keep the peace, she rose from her seat, and grabbed her purse. "I'm ready when you are."

Dante stood, slipped a hand possessively around her

waist and hugged her to his side. Jordana liked when he did that, loved how he made her feel safe and secure in his arms. Patting her affectionately on the hips, he lowered his mouth to her face, and she got a faint whiff of his aftershave. Jordana feared—and secretly hoped—he was going to kiss her. His voice was a gentle caress against her skin, arousing her flesh.

"The next few months will be nothing if not interesting." Dante dropped his mouth to her ear, and kissed her softly and tenderly on the cheek. "I can't wait."

Chapter 12

"We have to hurry, Mrs. Morretti, or the appetizers won't be ready by six o'clock."

Jordana hid the goofy, lopsided smile that overwhelmed her mouth. Every time someone inside the kitchen called her "Mrs. Morretti," her heart filled with pride. She'd been living at the estate for only three days, but she'd already learned the names of everyone on staff, cleaned and organized Matteo's bedroom and revised the weekly food plan. Dante ate like a frat boy, and since his poor eating habits were rubbing off on Matteo, she'd tossed out all the junk food in the pantry, then made a trip to the organic grocery store and stocked the fridge with fresh produce.

Opening the oven with one hand, Jordana slid the tray of stuffed potatoes inside, and set the timer. Blowing out a deep breath, she mentally reviewed her to-do list. Jordana felt as if she was living out an episode of a housewives series—minus the cat fights, four-hour lunch dates and endless glasses of booze. As she flitted around the kitchen, folding napkins and shining silverware, she fought the urge to pinch herself.

While Jordana chopped up the bell peppers, her mind wandered. In less than seventy-two hours her life had changed drastically. She'd married Dante, then after a scrumptious meal she'd moved into his mansion. It was the most exciting thing to ever happen to her. He was living the American dream, selling it, too. Everything about her new "husband" was flashy, ostentatious and over-the-top. Case in point: his ten-bedroom estate. It had everything she'd expect from a man as spoiled and as wealthy as Dante. Mosaic floors, vaulted ceilings dripping in gold, contemporary furnishings imported from his native Italy, a wine cellar and a man cave filled with more video games than an arcade.

Her gaze drifted to the window. The outdoor living room was decorated with vibrant pillows and comfy chairs. Tropical plants and flowers beautified the garden, and the heated pool looked so tempting she'd treated herself to a long, relaxing swim that morning. The estate had all the amenities of a five star hotel, and was by far the most lavish place she'd ever seen.

Her thoughts returned to Friday afternoon, and a dreamy sigh fell from her lips. After lunch, Dante had driven to Rodeo Drive, pulled up in front of Versace and handed over his platinum card. It was like a scene out of a Hollywood movie, and walking into the store on his arm gave Jordana a rush. Everyone—from the Barbie-thin clerks to the bejeweled shoppers—stared at them in amazement. To appease him, she'd tried on gowns fresh off the runway, glitzy high-heel shoes, eye-catching scarves and sunglasses, and even though it took supreme effort, she didn't argue when he insisted on buying everything in her dressing room.

Jordana smiled at the memory. Shopping didn't excite

her; touching him did. Walking down the sunny, tree-lined street, arm in arm, had given her a dizzying rush. His caress was thrilling, warmed her all over, and made her crave him more. Arriving at his estate hours later, Jordana was shocked to see a hot pink Bentley, wrapped in a ribbon, sitting in the driveway. He got a kick out of showing her the features inside the car. Test-driving the Bentley, she noticed how animated and excited he actually was. And when he suggested they park on Bel Air Road, and christen the backseat, she'd laughed out loud. Thinking about it now, she giggled.

"Jordana, is dinner ready? Something smells delicious, and I'm starving."

Facing him, her heart skipped a beat. *God, I hate when that happens. What's the matter with me? Why do I break into a cold sweat every time he flashes that thousand-watt grin?*

Because you're attracted to him, and you want him in your bed!

His stare was bold, sliding down her curves with erotic intent. Smartly dressed in a powder blue shirt and white pants, reclining comfortably on the couch, he looked like a Giorgio Armani model ready for his close-up. "You just ate."

He made his eyes wide, and patted his flat stomach. "I'm a growing boy."

"Growing boy, my ass," she quipped. "You're greedy and you know it."

"You're an actress, right? So, why don't you *act* like my wife, and fix me a plate?"

Feigning anger, Jordana narrowed her gaze, and shook her fist in the air. "Keep it up, buster, and the *only* thing you'll be eating is a knuckle sandwich."

His laughter echoed throughout the house, and Jordana heard the kitchen staff snicker.

"When is Mom coming back?" Matteo asked. "I miss her."

Jordana's ears perked up. For days, Matteo had been sad and withdrawn, but when she spoke to Dante about her concerns he'd shrugged them off. He said his son was tired from karate class and his other after-school activities, but Jordana wasn't convinced. That morning at Matteo's request, they'd called Lourdes and left a message on her voice mail. His mom was in rehab, but the least she could do was call and check in with her son.

Exiting the kitchen, with a plate of appetizers in each hand, Jordana marched into the living room determined to brighten Matteo's mood.

"Can I call my mom? I want to tell her about sports day and my graduation."

"Mom went away for a while, remember, li'l man?" Dante ruffled his curls, and kissed the top of his head. "She'll be back soon, but in the meantime you can hang out with me and Jordana. How does that sound?"

Matteo shrugged his bent shoulders. "Okay, I guess."

"Just 'okay'?" Dante tossed aside the remote control, and surged to his feet. His face was a dark mask, his hands were suspended in midair and he spoke in a creepy voice. "You're in big trouble, mister. The Claws of Doom are out, and I'm going to make you pay!"

Matteo's eyes widened with fear. "Not the Claws of Doom!"

"You're going down. You hear that, little boy? Your butt is mine."

"Someone save me!"

Dante grabbed Matteo, and tickled him until he begged for mercy. Shrieks of laughter filled the air, drowning out the classical music playing on the stereo system. And the louder Matteo screamed, the happier Jordana felt. Sure, he still missed his mother, but now he looked ecstatic, not dejected, and his dad was the reason why.

Jordana stood beside the bronze floor lamp, watching the adorable brown-eyed twosome, thinking there was nothing cuter than a father playing with his child. Seeing them together tugged at her heartstrings. Dante never ceased to amaze her. He had a keen mind for business, and had achieved incredible success in the real estate world. He had commercial and residential properties all across the state, not to mention vacation homes in Manhattan, Aspen and Palm Springs. But Jordana wasn't impressed with his vast real estate portfolio or his staggering net worth. She was impressed by how much he loved and adored his son. Matteo was his priority, not an afterthought, and she admired him for putting his child first. *He could teach my dad a thing or two about being a father, that's for sure.*

The doorbell chimed, and Jordana froze. Mr. Quan was early, but the main course was still in the oven. Glancing at the security camera mounted to the living room wall, she sighed in relief. It was Markos, and he looked dashing in an all-white ensemble.

"Yahoo! Uncle Markos is here, and he's taking me to the circus!" He leaped off the couch, and sprinted down the hall. "This is the moment I've been waiting for my entire life!"

Everyone in the room laughed—even the steely-eyed housekeeper dusting the shelves—but Dante wore a troubled expression on his face. His fingers were intertwined, clasped behind his head, and tension radiated from his body. She sensed his inner turmoil, and feared he was thinking about his ex-wife. *Does he miss Lourdes, too? Does he regret the divorce, and want to reunite with her for the sake of his son? Is he strategizing how to win her back?*

To pull him out of his thoughts, Jordana touched his shoulder and gestured to the gold-rimmed plate in her hands topped with delicious appetizers. "Eat up," she said, hiding a self-incriminating smile. "You're a growing boy who needs his strength, remember?"

"You've got jokes."

"Nope," she said, her tone cheeky. "Just fulfilling my duties as an obedient wife."

"Ha! If that's what you call obedience then I'm in serious trouble!"

Jordana burst out laughing. She loved his sense of humor, their playful banter, how easy it was to be around him. Dante took the plate from her hands, and caressed her fingers. The scent of their attraction filled the air, swirling around them. She opened her mouth, to ask which wine to serve with the first course, but lost her voice when his fingers traveled up her wrist.

Worried her legs would buckle, and she'd wipe out in her silk Givenchy dress, Jordana sat down on the armrest, and crossed her legs. Hearing loud, animated voices in the foyer, she peered down the hallway. Markos was holding Matteo in his arms, and the preschooler was giggling with glee. "Matteo's going to have a blast tonight," she said, smiling to herself. "That's nice of Markos to take him to the circus. What a sweetheart!"

"If you say so." Dante tasted an oyster, and chewed slowly, as if he was savoring each bite. "Markos says Matteo is a great wingman, so his motives are less than pure."

"I'm not surprised. After all, he *is* a Morretti."

"What's that supposed to mean? And why are you taking shots at my people?"

"No offense, but when it comes to the opposite sex the men in your family have a horrible reputation. Your cousins Demetri, Nicco and Rafael are on the celebrity blogs 24/7, and yesterday at the grocery store I saw pictures of your brother Emilio on the cover of the *National Equistar*. Apparently, he hooked up with a South African model at a yacht in Ibiza, and now she's claiming to be pregnant with his love child."

"Bullshit! Emilio's crazy about Sharleen and he'd never do anything to hurt her. Furthermore, he's too busy training around the clock to party. When he's not on the track he's at home romancing Sharleen. I spoke to him yesterday. He's so in love it's sickening!"

"Is Emilio meeting you in Tampa for the charity golf tournament?"

"He better, or that'll be his ass!"

The more Dante cracked jokes about his cousins and brothers, the harder she laughed.

"Can we listen to something else? Bach is putting me to sleep."

"No, we cannot," Jordana said, faking a British accent. "Hip-hop music isn't appropriate for a dinner party, and I seriously doubt Mr. Quan is a fan."

Dante scowled, made a puppy-dog face. "Party pooper!"

Spotting the servers standing at attention in front of the breakfast bar, Jordana sprung to her feet, straightened her dress and smoothed a hand over her silky locks. To please him she'd straightened her hair, selected one of the short figure-hugging gowns he'd bought her and donned turquoise accessories. From the moment she'd exited the guest bedroom, he'd been plying her with compliments, staring at her with lust in his eyes.

"There's the most beautiful woman in Bel Air."

Markos whistled. "Fantastic dress. Versace, right?"

"Yeah," she said slowly, raising an eyebrow. "How did you know?"

"I bought it for my ex. It looked nice on her, but it looks sensational on you."

Jordana beamed, and did a small twirl. "Boy, tell me something I don't know!"

Catching sight of the time on the wall clock, she waved

goodbye, and hustled into the kitchen as fast as her high heels could take her. Busy setting the table with Ralph Lauren lines, Jordana didn't notice Markos and Matteo were gone until she spotted them leaving the estate on the security cameras. When the doorbell rang an hour later, the seven-course Italian meal was cooling on top of the oven. The air held a savory aroma that made her mouth water and her stomach grumble, and Bach had been swapped for the late, great Whitney Houston.

"It's showtime." Coming up behind her, Dante took her hand, raised it to his mouth and kissed it. "This is the biggest deal of my career, and I need you to make me look good tonight. Think you can you handle that, Mrs. Morretti?"

"Absolutely," she insisted, wearing her game face. "And to thank me for a job well done you're taking me to see *Madame Butterfly* at the LA Opera next Sunday."

Dante groaned, and hung his head. "No way. *Anything* but the opera."

The butler, a bald Irishman with eyeglasses, entered the room and stood at attention, his hands clasped rigidly behind his back. "Introducing Lu Quan and Sunny Zhang."

Born in Hong Kong and educated in France, the Chinese billionaire was one of the most influential businessmen in the world. But his short stature, spiky hair and designer shades made him look more like the front man for a rock band than a fifty-year-old real estate giant.

"This is so exciting! I can't believe this is actually happening."

Sunny threw her arms around Jordana, and hugged her so tight she felt her bones crack. The petite brunette radiated warmth and positive energy, and her frilly peach dress made her skin glow. Her accent was thick, but her excitement was palpable.

"I've been to LA several times, but I've never met a

real-life actress before," she said with a giggle. "My girlfriends are going to squeal when I tell them I met you!"

Puzzled, she shot Dante a what-the-hell-is-going-on look. He wore a broad grin, and Jordana knew he'd lied to the couple about her acting credentials.

"What movies have you starred in? I'm a huge movie buff, but I'm embarrassed to say I don't recognize you from anything."

"Don't be, Mr. Quan. I haven't been in anything besides a few TV commercials—"

"Remember her name," Dante advised, cutting her off. "Because it's just a matter of time before my beautiful new bride becomes a bona fide Hollywood superstar."

"I believe it, Dante, and you're right, she's stunning."

"Likewise, Mr. Quan. It looks like we *both* hit the jackpot on our wedding day."

The men laughed, and the women nodded in agreement.

"Can we speak in private? It's important."

Sunny glared at her husband, but she spoke to him in a soft, soothing voice. "Honey, but we just got here. Can't you discuss business later? After we've socialized?"

"Let them go." Jordana linked arms with Sunny, and patted her forearm. "We'll have cocktails and appetizers and gossip about them behind their backs. How does that sound?"

"Scandalous!" Sunny giggled, and waved. "See ya, boys!"

Laughing, the women marched off, their high heels clicking loudly on the marble floor.

Dante tracked Jordana's movements with his eyes. He didn't have the strength to turn away, didn't even try. She always knew what to say to put people at ease, and her enthusiasm was contagious. He loved Tavares, thought he was wise beyond his years, but dumping Jordana was the dumbest thing he'd ever done. No doubt about it. She was the total package, everything a man could want—compassionate, loyal, honest and trustworthy. Not to mention drop-dead sexy. Her gown was tasteful, her vibrant accessories gave her outfit a splash of color, and her ankle-tie sandals drew attention to her long, silky legs—legs he wished were clamped around his waist. With her in that clingy dress and those red do-me-hard pumps, it was going to be impossible for him to be a gentleman tonight. *I have to have her. By any means necessary.*

His thoughts returned to yesterday. During breakfast, she'd given him a forty-minute lecture about family and the importance of being a man of integrity. He'd then decided against going to Morretti Realty and drove the eighty miles to Big Bear Lake instead. It turned out to be a wise decision. They'd done it all—hiking, fishing and even horseback riding. Dante didn't know anyone who loved the great outdoors as much as Jordana did, and he was amazed by her get-up-and-go attitude. He was happy Jordana and Matteo were close, found it amusing to watch them together, but the next time they went out of town he was leaving his son at home. He wanted to be alone with Jordana, without Matteo dragging her off to play. As he admired her delicious backside, he made a mental note to plan a special trip for her.

It took supreme effort, but he tore his gaze away from her ass and gave Mr. Quan his undivided attention. Wanting privacy, he showed the Chinese businessman to his office, gestured to the leather bucket chairs in front of the window and took a seat. "What is on your mind, sir? Would you like to discuss the development deal in Sheung Wan?"

"What were you thinking?"

Taken aback by the billionaire's harsh tone, Dante took a moment to gather his thoughts, and leaned forward in his chair. "Sir, I'm afraid I don't know what you are talking about."

"Two strippers showed up at my suite at The Peninsula Beverly Hills as my wife and I were getting ready for your dinner party." His eyes darkened. "I called Mr. Smirnov, and he apologized on your behalf. He promised to give you a stern talking-to tomorrow morning. But I felt it was important to speak to you man-to-man."

Staggered, as if he'd been whacked upside the head with a pot, Dante couldn't speak.

"I wasn't going to come tonight, but Sunny was desperate to meet your wife so I relented. If you ever pull a stunt like that again I'll bury you. I won't let you humiliate me..."

Dante wore a blank expression on his face, but inside he was seething with anger. His boss had disregarded his advice, screwed up, then pinned the blame on him. Was this payback for not dropping Ryder Knoxx as a client? Was this Mr. Smirnov's way of getting even with him? By ruining his reputation?

"Sir, I did not send strippers to your suite."

"You didn't? But Mr. Smirnov said you did."

Dante clutched the armrest, but he wished he was wringing his boss's neck. Taking a deep breath, he masked his emotions with a confident smile. "I know you're a devout Christian, and I'd never do anything to disrespect you or your faith."

"I'm glad to hear that, because I don't do business with deceitful people."

Then stay far *away from Mr. Smirnov because he's a snake in Armani!*

"The Brokerage Group isn't the right fit for me."

Dante was mad, pissed at his boss for betraying him, but he wasn't going to lose the biggest deal of his career. Not without a fight. "Sir, I know you're upset, but please don't make any hasty decisions. The Brokerage Group is one of the most widely recognized names in real estate with offices all around the world. In a survey by *Real Estate Trends*, a leading resource for international real estate rankings, TBG claimed the top ten spots."

"Can I be frank?"

Curious to hear more, Dante nodded, and leaned forward expectantly in his chair.

"Much of my success is due to my intuition, and my gut is telling me to walk away, and fast. I don't know much about Mr. Smirnov, but from what I've seen, he's an unscrupulous businessman with no conscience. I don't trust him."

"I understand."

"That being said I respect you, and admire the way you handle yourself. You're a smart, astute go-getter and I want to do business with your company, Morretti Realty."

Dante was pleased, grateful for the compliment, but he grappled over what to do. Doing business with Mr. Quan could cost him his job—and more important his reputation—and he'd worked too damn hard, for too damn long, to lose everything. "Take a couple weeks to think about it, and let me know what you decide."

"Thank you, sir. I will."

"Don't be so formal. Call me Lu." Raising his eyebrows, he cocked his head to the right, and sniffed the air. "Is that scaloppini catanese I smell? And garlic ciabatta bread?"

"Yes, it is, and I'm glad you enjoy fine cuisine because my beautiful wife made an authentic Italian meal. It's waiting for us in the main-floor dining room."

Lu jumped to his feet. "Then why are we sitting here? Let's eat!"

Chapter 13

"Have you ever dated one of your A-list costars on the down low?"

The question caught Jordana off guard, but she didn't let her surprise show on her face. Thanks to Dante, their dinner guests thought she was an up-and-coming actress, and nothing she said could change their mind. Sunny and Lu were an adorable couple, eager to learn about Western culture and proud to share facts about their native country. For the past hour they'd been grilling her about Hollywood and all things celebrity. "No, never, and now that I'm a happily married woman there's no chance of that ever happening."

"Good answer, baby." Dante kissed her lips. "You're mine, all mine, and I'm yours."

God, how I wish that was true! Jordana understood. Knew the score. They were newlyweds. They were supposed to be touchy-feely, but her heart—and her body—couldn't take it anymore. All the gazing and caressing, flirting and smiling had gotten to her, and now all she could think about was making love. Her body desperately wanted and craved sex. She doubted a cold shower would cool her raging hormones.

Conversation was loud and spirited, full of jokes and hearty laughs. The evening passed so quickly Jordana couldn't believe the time on the grandfather clock. She had to be up at 7:00 a.m. to make Matteo breakfast, but she was having fun with their lively, well-heeled guests, and sleep was the last thing on her mind. Matteo had returned home during dessert, chatting a mile a minute about his outing to the circus. His clown impersonation had left the group in stitches. After a warm bubble bath, he'd hopped into his car bed and had fallen fast asleep.

"When did you know you were destined to be a star?" Sunny asked, her eyes bright with interest. "How did it happen? Did your parents see that special spark in you early on?"

Discussing her childhood always made Jordana feel melancholy, but she spoke with a smile. Not all of her memories were sad, and as she reflected on that cold winter night decades earlier, her spirits brightened. "When I was eight years old, I snuck into my parents' bedroom and hid in the closet while they were watching *Antonella*," she confessed. "I knew right then and there that I wanted to be an actress, and nothing my father said could change my mind. He still wants me to return to school and finish up my education degree, but my heart just isn't in it."

Dante furrowed his thick, perfectly groomed eyebrows. "What's *Antonella*?"

"Only the greatest story ever told!" Jordana quipped. "It's a Cuban love story about a forbidden romance. I've watched it so many times I know the dialogue by heart!"

Wearing a blissful expression on her face, Sunny snuggled against her husband. "It sounds like my kind of movie. Maybe we'll watch it tonight when we return to the hotel."

"You're going to love it," Jordana promised. "I've seen *Antonella* a million times, but the ending is so touching and romantic it always brings me to tears."

Soon, the men were discussing sports and politics, leaving the women to trade beauty tips and recipes. Aside from Waverly, and a couple of colleagues at LA Marketing, Jordana had few friends, so having dinner with a worldly, urbane socialite was an honor. "Does anyone want more wine? Coffee? Tiramisu?"

"No, thank you. Nothing for me." Lu pulled back his shirt sleeve, and showed his wife his Rolex watch. "We should go. It's late, and you know how I get if don't get sufficient sleep."

Sunny smirked. "He's a bear in Armani, and that's putting it nicely."

"I feel your pain. So is Dante!"

Dante wore an exaggerated frown, and the women cracked up.

"You must come to Hong Kong soon. I know our friends and family would love to meet you, and I'd be proud to show you around my beloved hometown."

"Sunny, that's a great idea. I've been contemplating where to take Jordana for our belated honeymoon, but I never considered a trip overseas."

"You should definitely come out east," she encouraged, tossing her silk shawl dramatically over her shoulders. "What's not to love about Hong Kong? We have it all. A rich history and culture, delectable food and gracious people, and the designer boutiques along Causeway Road put Rodeo Drive to shame."

"In that case, can we leave tomorrow?"

"Absolutely, baby. Anything for you." Dante draped an arm around her chair and drew his fingers slowly across her shoulders. Gazing at him, she felt that familiar pull drawing her to him. Marrying him had been a wise decision, quite possibly the smartest thing she'd ever done. He was a Renaissance man with many skills and talents, and Jordana was in awe. Blown away by his inherent charm and charisma, she couldn't look at Dante without fantasizing about kissing him passionately, over and over and over again.

That's not all *you want to do!* teased her inner voice.

"Thank you for a wonderful evening." Lu rose from his seat and helped his wife out of her chair. "We'll be sure to return the favor when you come to Hong Kong."

"We'd love that."

Jordana gave Sunny a hug. "Don't be a stranger. You have my contact information, so please keep in touch."

"I will, and good luck on your auditions next week. Knock them dead!"

Walking their guests through the main floor to the foyer, Jordana realized she was sad to see them go. Sunny invited them to visit their family estate in The Peak, an exclusive suburb in Hong Kong teeming with celebrities and million-dollar homes. Dante promised to make it happen. Jordana hated flying, got violently ill whenever she did, and shuddered at the thought of spending sixteen hours on a plane. But she had nodded in agreement.

Standing on the steps with Dante, she watched the happy couple climb into their chauffeured Mercedes SUV, and waved as it exited the estate.

"You were incredible tonight. Hospitable, engaging, gracious and sweet," Dante praised, his tone and his expression one of pride. "And you can really throw down in the kitchen. I didn't realize I'd married a world-class chef until I tasted your mushroom fusilli!"

Jordana burst out laughing. She couldn't believe Dante of all people had enjoyed her food.

"You've been holding out on me."

"I'm a woman of many talents."

"That you are, and I look forward to discovering each and every one of them."

He was flirting with her, bold in his approach, and Jordana liked it. Liked that he knew what he wanted, and wasn't afraid to speak his mind. For as long as she could remember, she'd always had a thing for suave, cocky guys, and Dante was no exception. The more time they spent together—experimenting in the kitchen, swimming with Matteo in the family pool, working out at the gym—the more comfortable Jordana felt playing his wife. She was looking forward to their movie date tomorrow night with Markos and his on-again, off-again surgeon girlfriend.

"I didn't know you had auditions coming up until Sunny mentioned it. Why didn't you say anything?" he asked, touching a hand to her waist.

"Because I didn't want you to tease me."

"Why? You're not auditioning for a *SpongeBob SquarePants* cartoon are you?"

"No, a music video for Renegade's new single, 'On Fleek.' If you make fun of me, I'm going to knock you out," she joked.

"When did you start auditioning for music videos?"

"I usually don't, but Fallon asked me to give it a try, and I agreed." Remembering the conversation she'd had with her agent yesterday, she said, "Lots of movie stars got their start on the small screen. Angelina Jolie, Halle Berry and Julia Roberts have all been in music videos. Since they've all won Oscars, I think landing the part could open a lot of doors for me."

"Yeah, *bedroom* doors." His eyes darkened with anger. "I don't like Renegade's music."

"Well, I do," she said, refusing to let Dante dampen her spirits. Her agent was friends with the director, and there was a good chance she'd be one of the five girls selected for the shoot. "And since the pay is fantastic, I'll be there bright and early Friday morning."

"Jordana, you don't need to work. All you need to do is look good on my arm, take care of Matteo and ensure everything is running smoothly here at the estate."

Her toes curled inside her pumps. His words bothered her, but she kept her temper in check. They'd had a wonderful evening, and she didn't want to ruin it by arguing with Dante about her acting career. Sure, he gave great advice, and supported her wholeheartedly, but Fallon knew the business better than anyone and Jordana was going to trust her.

"Dante, simmer down. Don't get your tighty whities in a bunch..."

He cracked a smile, and Jordana knew he was eating out of the palm of her hand.

"It's just an audition. I don't have the part yet. Besides, the chances of Renegade picking me are slim to none. There'll be hundreds of young, tantalizing beauties there, and as your son so aptly pointed out this afternoon while we were playing soccer, I'm *way* old."

"He's four. Don't listen to him. You don't look a day over twenty-nine," he said, with a sly grin.

Jordana stuck out her tongue. "Thanks. You're too kind."

"Just calling it like I see it." He reached out, and touched her hair. "I miss your curls."

"You do? I thought you'd prefer something more mainstream and less Bohemian chic. Isn't that what you wanted?"

"No, not at all. I always want you to be you. Curls and all."

Her eyebrows shot up. "I'm confused."

"I screwed up, and I'm sorry. I didn't mean to hurt your

feelings, or make you think you're not good enough. I was worried about you being photographed at thrift stores and garage sales, but I went about it the wrong way."

His tone was full of warmth and sincerity, and she sensed he was telling her the truth. "Is that all it was? Thank God. I thought you hated my style."

"You couldn't be more wrong. I love your look."

"You do?"

"Isn't it obvious? I've been staring at you all night. If we didn't have company, I would have ripped your dress off and made love to you on the dining-room table *twice*."

The expression on his face, and his bold declaration, shook her to the core, leaving her breathless. His gaze was filled with lust, and pierced her flesh with desire.

"I've wanted you from the moment I first saw you."

Blown away, she listened with rapt attention, her eyes wide and her mouth agape.

"You were dating my friend," he said, his voice resigned. "I didn't want to do anything to disrespect him or your relationship, so I kept my distance. But my feelings for you never changed...haven't changed... I want you now more than ever."

His hands moved down her neck, over her shoulders and along her hips. His caress aroused her. Excited her. Made her heart dance and her knees weak. Her temperature rose, warming her skin, and her breasts swelled under her designer gown. Desperate for his touch, the thought of his skillful tongue against her flesh caused her nipples to harden.

"We're going to renegotiate the terms of our deal, right here, right now."

Jordana couldn't get her thoughts in order, or her mouth to work. She didn't know when or how it happened, but her body was pressed against his, and her hands were draped around his neck. Her gaze slid down his physique and zeroed in on the wide bulge in his pants. She felt his erection against her thighs, and moved closer. Dante oozed sex appeal from every pore, and she had a hell of a time keeping her eyes on his face and off his crotch. Her mouth was wet, salivating at the thought of his naked body, and her hands itched to touch him. Jordana wanted Dante between her legs, pleasing her, stroking her—

Jordana pressed her eyes shut, and dropped her hands to her sides. "No. We can't. Things will get complicated and messy and I don't want to ruin our friendship."

"That will never happen," he said in a strong, convincing tone. "I won't let it."

Jordana clamped her lips together to prevent the truth from spilling out. If she was being honest with herself, she'd always had feelings for Dante—romantic, sexual feelings she struggled to control whenever he was nearby—and that would likely never change. From the day they'd met he'd had a reoccurring role in her dreams and dominated her every thought. Isn't that why she'd lied to Tavares about being celibate? She wanted sex, just not with him. He was a nice enough guy—successful, ambitious, from a great family—but he didn't light her fire. Not the way Dante did. Truth be told, when Tavares dumped her, she'd felt relieved, not sad, and had secretly hoped to one day have a chance with Dante. Here it was, her opportunity to come clean, but she couldn't do it. Baring her soul was risky, and she'd rather be alone than take a chance on love.

"Are you attracted to me?"

"I'm attracted to a lot of people," she lied, faking bravado.

"That's not what I asked you."

Jordana tapped the face of her watch. "Oh, wow, look at the time. I'm going to finish up in the kitchen then go to bed. Sleep well, Dante. See you in the morning!"

Spinning around, her heart beating erratically, her legs wobbling, she took off down the hall. She didn't get far.

Dante grabbed her around the waist, thwarting her escape. He led her into the living room, sat down on the couch and pulled her down onto his lap. "You're not going anywhere. The kitchen staff will clean up. That's their job."

"I sent them home after dessert."

His hands caressed her legs, slowly moving up her thighs. "Smart move. Now we don't have to worry about anyone interrupting us."

"What are you doing?"

"Fulfilling my marital vows. I promised to cherish you, and that's what I'm going to do."

Heat burned her cheeks, spread from her ears to her toes. Jordana couldn't resist him. Not tonight. Not when he looked at her like *that*, and showered her with compliments and praise. Overwhelmed with explicit thoughts—thoughts of sexing him in every room of the estate—her breathing sped up, and her heartbeat roared in her ears.

"Do you want me?"

Yes! Yes! Yes! Let's do *this!*

The truth must have showed on her face, because he crushed his lips to her mouth and devoured them. Over and over again he kissed her. Passionately, fervently, urgently, as if his next breath depended on it. *I must be dreaming. This can't be real.* But his hand inside her panties was *very* real, kindling her body's fire with every stroke.

"You're wet for me," he said, between kisses. "I like…"

A moan fell from her lips, then another. He probed her sex, moved his nimble fingers in a deliciously slow rhythm. He was turning her out, using everything in his arsenal to excite her, and she loved every minute of it. She rode his fingers, bucked against them, gripped his hand to control the pace. Her first time—a painful, five-minute romp with a college freshman at a raucous frat party—was a disaster and Jordana wished she could erase it from her memory. Since she couldn't she'd do the next best thing. Have her way with Dante. Tonight, Jordana was calling the shots. She would be in complete control. She wasn't a shy, timid virgin anymore; she was the bold, sexy teacher. She knew what she liked, what she wanted, and it was Dante.

Grabbing his shirt collar, she kissed him hard on the mouth. Jordana was stunned by the savage intensity of the kiss, but didn't stop licking and sucking his lips. She kissed him harder. Deeper. With the passion flowing through her veins. She made love to him with her mouth, nibbled on it as if it were fruit.

Draping her arms around his neck, she dug her hands into his hair, rubbing and massaging his scalp. He groaned, and her heart soared with pride. Suddenly, her dress felt restrictive, tighter than a straitjacket, so she unzipped it. Pushing it down her hips, she tossed it on the floor. A devilish grin covered his face. He made her feel sexy, desirable, and it was the ultimate turn-on.

"That was my job."

"You were taking too long."

"I thought you didn't want me. Didn't want this."

"And I thought you were an astute businessman skilled at reading between the lines."

"Come here, and I'll show you just how *skilled* I am."

Dante turned her over on her stomach, cupped her breasts from behind and blew a warm breath against the base of her ear. Pleasure careened down her spine. He sprayed kisses across her neck, shoulders and along her back. Not knowing where his lips would end up next made her body tingle with anticipation. Starting at her toes, he worked his way up her legs to her thighs, stroked, caressed and licked her as if pleasing her was his sole mission in life.

"You have a beautiful ass." Dante lowered his mouth to her bottom, and pressed a kiss to each plump cheek. "It's round and tight, and I love how it fits perfectly in my hands."

"Is that all you love?" she teased, tossing a coy smile over her shoulder.

"No, I love everything."

"Don't tell me. Show me." Hearing the words leave her mouth, her eyes widened. She'd never been this bold with a lover, but Dante made her feel alive and confident. Since tonight was about letting go, she ripped the shirt from his chest, and yanked it down his shoulders. To show how much she desired him, she kissed from his neck to his nipples and his six-pack. There was nothing she wouldn't do for Dante, and pleasing him was the only thing on her mind. Unzipping his pants, she slid a hand inside his boxer briefs. He was well endowed, and she trembled at the sight of his long, stiff erection. At a loss for words, all she could do was stare. And drool.

"I love your lips…your breasts…your legs…and right here." He slid his erection against her sex, moving it back and forth, up and down. "I love *this* the most."

His pulse-pounding smile, coupled with his piercing gaze, pushed her over the edge. Scared she'd scream, and wake up the entire neighborhood, she pressed her lips together, trapping a moan inside. This was heaven. Nirvana. The only place in the world she wanted to be.

"Baby, are you okay? Is it too deep? Do you want me to stop?"

"If you do, I'll kill you!"

"Spoken like a true Aries," he shot back, with a hearty chuckle.

"I've fantasized about this moment for weeks, and I don't want it to end."

"If that's how you felt, then why didn't you make the first move?"

It was hard to think straight, with his fingers playing between her legs, tickling and swirling around in her curls, but she gave her head a shake, and forced her lips to move.

"Because we're friends and I didn't want things to be awkward between us if things went south."

"Is that all I am to you? Just a friend?"

"What would you like to be?"

"Your everything..."

He kissed the tip of her nose, the corners of her lips, pressing his mouth to her earlobe. Jordana shivered. *To have and to hold* had taken on a whole new meaning, and for as long as she lived she'd never forget how cherished and adored he'd made her feel tonight. She opened her mouth to suggest they go upstairs to his suite, but it was too late. One swift thrust and Dante was inside her, pumping his legs and swiveling his hips. It was the most erotic moment of her life, and Jordana knew she'd be reliving it for years to come.

Their lovemaking was fast and furious, fraught with lust, and as they moved together as one—one mind, one body, one heart—she clung desperately to him. Dante took her to heights and depths she'd never experienced. To a world filled with vivid lights and colors and music, and when he whispered naughty words in her ears, passion erupted inside her body.

Jordana was lost. Out of it. In anothcr stratosphcrc. Experiencing an earth-shattering orgasm that knocked the wind out of her. She tried to control the trembling in her limbs, but pleasure shot to her core, and she cried out for the second time in minutes.

Her head spinning out of control, Jordana collapsed against the sofa cushions. She'd never climaxed that fast, but before she could catch her breath another one hit. But, still, it wasn't enough. Greedy for more, she spread her legs wide, and thrust her hips against his erection, pulling him deeper inside.

"You like that, baby?"

"Do. I. Ever."

"Jordana, I'm all in. All yours. There will never be anyone else for me. Only you."

"That's the champagne talking," she teased, determined to keep her wits about her. Now was not the time to overthink things, to start talking and acting crazy. This was sex—incredible, passionate, mind-blowing—and nothing more.

"I'm not drunk."

Jordana tenderly caressed his face. "No promises, okay? Let's just enjoy tonight."

"One night just won't do." Gazing down at her, he slid his hands across her back and roughly grabbed her ass. "You're the most enthusiastic lover I've ever had, and I just can't get enough. The more I have, the more I want."

"It's easy to be enthusiastic when I'm with you. You're amazing."

"Keep talking like that, and I'm going to lock you up and throw away the key!"

"Please do." Jordana sucked his nipple into her mouth, hungrily, as if it were smothered in chocolate and he was her favorite dessert. "I could definitely get used to this."

He pressed his eyes shut, thrusting harder, deeper, filling her sex with his delicious length. His head fell back, and groans and grunts streamed out of his lips, filling the air. Sweat dripped from his brow, and he was breathing heavily as if he'd just finished a marathon. His face tensed, then his body went perfectly still. Jordana expected Dante to collapse onto the couch, and fall asleep, but he surprised her. He stood, in all his masculine glory, scooped her up in his arms, and cradled her to his chest. "Where are we going?"

"Upstairs."

"Are you tired?"

"No," he said slyly. "That was the warm-up. Now it's time for the main event."

Jordana licked her lips. "Let the games begin!"

Chapter 14

Jordana awoke with a jolt, bolted upright in bed and rubbed the sleep from her eyes. Sunshine spilled into the master bedroom through the wide-open French doors, filling the elegantly decorated suite with light, and the warm breeze carried a floral scent.

Taking in her posh surroundings, Jordana realized two things at once: it wasn't a dream. She had, in fact, sexed Dante *all* night long, and two, she'd overslept and missed breakfast with Matteo—her favorite part of the day.

Groaning, she tossed aside the gold satin sheets, and dragged her aching body out of the king-size bed. A gasp fell from her lips. She was naked and there were traces of chocolate and whip cream between her thighs.

Shame burned her cheeks, surging through her veins. Searching frantically for her dress, Jordana chastised herself for succumbing to her desires and having unprotected sex with Dante. How many times *had* they made love?

Three, four, five times? Delirious with need, she'd lost count of how many orgasms she'd had.

Jordana thought hard for several seconds, and everything came flooding back—flirting with Dante during dinner, ripping off his clothes, the climax that stole her breath. It was the most thrilling, romantic night of her life. His tender kisses, caresses and heartfelt words touched her soul, proved they had a special bond that could never be broken. And the sex was toe-curling, spine-tingling, smack-your-mama good. So good, in fact, it was all Jordana could think about.

"There you are. I thought you'd never wake up…"

Startled to hear Dante's voice behind her, Jordana snatched a pillow off the bed, covered her body and spun around. He looked hot in his black Nike jacket and nylon shorts. Her mouth watered at the sight of him. "Where are my clothes?"

"Good morning to you, too."

"Dante, knock it off. This isn't funny," she snapped, glancing at the digital alarm clock positioned on the mahogany dresser. "School started thirty minutes ago, and I still have to pack Matteo's lunch, and iron his uniform."

"Baby, relax."

"Relax?" she repeated, shouting the word. "Didn't you hear what I just said? Because of me Matteo's late for school, and now there's a good chance Ms. Papadopoulos will make good on her threat and contact Child and Family Services—"

"No, she won't. I made Matteo breakfast, packed him a healthy lunch *and* I dropped him off early." His smile was proud, tinged with mischief. "How you like me now?"

Jordana released a deep sigh. "Thanks, Dante. You're a lifesaver."

"What's up with the pillow?"

"What pillow?"

He pointed at her hands. "The one you're clutching for dear life."

"I can't find my dress, and I've looked everywhere."

"Who needs clothes when you have a body like *that*?"

Heat rose up her neck, singed her cheeks and ears. He was teasing her, of course, feeding her one of his many winning lines, so why was her heart fluttering around inside her chest like a monarch butterfly? And why was she filled with an overwhelming sense of love and gratitude?

"I've seen every inch of your gorgeous, delectable shape, and you have nothing to be ashamed of. You should be damn proud. Your body is a beautiful masterpiece."

Dodging his gaze, she stared at the framed portraits displayed on the black-and-white walls of his master suite. Seeing her refection in the dresser mirror, Jordana groaned inwardly. *Masterpiece? Right. More like a freakin' disaster!* Last night, she'd sweated out her perm. Her hair was now a tangled frizzy mess in desperate need of a flatiron. But her eyes were clear and bright, and a radiant glow colored her skin. She felt changed somehow, different after their sexual encounter, and smiled to herself at the memory of their first time.

"Do you regret making love?"

"Yes...no... I don't know," she blurted out, tightening her grip on the pillow. Her heart thumped inside her chest, throbbing loudly in her ears. For some inexplicable reason, she'd lost her voice. She couldn't think or speak. Jordana felt ridiculous for using the pillow as a shield, but she didn't want Dante to see her naked. Silly, considering they'd made love several times. But Jordana couldn't change her feelings, or control her quivering limbs.

"Baby, let's talk." He unzipped his lightweight jacket, chucked it on the couch and kicked off his crisp all-white sneakers. "Would it make you feel better if I got naked, too?"

"Dante, can you be serious for once? This isn't funny."

He strode into the walk-in-closet, which was bigger than her former apartment, and returned seconds later carrying a silk robe with the word *Morretti* inscribed above the pocket. Ever the gentleman, he placed it on the bed, and turned toward window. The gesture touched her heart, and as Jordana slipped it on over her shoulders, the faint scent of his Yves Saint Laurent aftershave washed over her, calming her frazzled nerves.

"Better now?" he asked, taking her hand in his.

Nodding, Jordana dropped her gaze to the carpet, and studied her fuchsia toes. She felt his eyes on her, watching her, and sank onto the bed. "Dante, for the record, I'm not mad at you. I'm mad at myself."

"Why? For doing something we've both wanted for months?"

"Dante, this isn't me. I've never had a one-night stand, and I don't have casual sex."

"Good, because I don't want to compete with anyone else for your heart. I want you all to myself." He sat beside her, wrapped her up in his arms and kissed her forehead. "Last night wasn't a mistake. I'm glad we made love, and I have no regrets."

"Of course you don't. You're a guy, a Morretti at that."

"There you go insulting my family again. What's up with that?"

"You said marriage is hell on earth, so it would be stupid of me to think we'll ride off into the sunset, and live happily ever after in this estate."

He cocked an eyebrow, wore a what-are-you-talking-about expression on his face.

"What?" Raising her hands in the air, as if surrendering to the LAPD, she opened her eyes wide. "Don't get mad at me. They're your words, not mine."

"Bullshit. I never said that."

"Yes, you did."

Dante dropped his hands from her shoulders to his lap. "When?"

"During Markos's New Year's Eve bash. You said relationships sucked, and the only way you'd ever get remarried was if a loaded gun was pointed to your head." On a roll, she repeated their conversation word for word. "I thought you were kidding, but you sounded dead serious."

"I didn't mean it. I had too much to drink and ran my mouth. Don't hold it against me."

Jordana pushed a hand through her hair, felt a golf ball–sized knot and wanted to kick herself in the teeth for throwing herself at him last night. She had hair from hell and sore limbs. Worse still, she couldn't get her thoughts out of the gutter. Every time Dante looked at her, she wanted to dive into his arms, rip the clothes from his muscled body and ride him like a pony.

Good job, girl. You've created a fine mess this time.

"I married you to win custody of Matteo, but I knew it was just a matter of time before we became lovers. I've always wanted you, and after last night I want you even more."

Aroused by his words, and his gentle caress along her arms and hips, it became impossible for Jordana to focus. Her mind returned to last night and her nipples hardened, aching to be squeezed, sucked and licked. Recalling how amazing his tongue had felt between her legs caused tremors to rock her body. Jordana deleted the image from her mind and returned to the conversation, desperate to make Dante understand why they couldn't be lovers.

"I'm not the only one who loves sex," he teased. "So do you. I was exhausted when we stumbled into bed this morning, but you were raring to go and had your way with me, *twice*."

So, we did make love four *times!* Jordana held his stare.

She couldn't hide her dreamy gaze, or the grin that claimed her mouth. "Are you complaining?"

"Never. We have great conversations about life, incredible chemistry and the loving is on point. But our relationship is about more than just sex."

Dante touched her cheek, slowly caressing it with his thumb, and she nuzzled her face against his strong, warm hand. Jordana heard the vacuum outside the bedroom door, and wondered if the middle-aged housekeeper, who acted more like his mother than his employee, was spying on them or actually doing her job.

"Your friendship has changed me for the better," he confessed. "I'm not perfect, and I still lose my temper sometimes, but I've come a long way since the divorce, and you're the reason why. You're a breath of fresh air, and I love when you're around. So does Matteo."

Jordana held her breath and leaned into him. She waited for him to say the words her heart was longing to hear. It was an outrageous thought, considering they'd slept together for the first time last night, but her feelings for Dante were real and she wanted to be the only woman in his life.

His cell phone rang, and he took it out of his pocket. "It's my boss. Do you mind if I take this call?"

Jordana shook her head. "Of course not."

"I'll meet you downstairs. We can have lunch together on the deck."

"Sounds great. I'll be down in a few."

Dante strode out of the suite with his cell to his ear, and disappeared down the hall.

Flopping back onto the bed, she sighed deeply, and stared up at the ceiling. Jordana felt empty inside, confused by their conversation, and wondered if she'd imagined the way he'd looked at her, his touch, the sweet and wonderful things he'd said as they'd made love. No, it was real. He'd said everything—except those three magic words—but Jordana chose to focus on the positives instead. They'd made love last night, opened up to each other like never before, and things could only get better from there.

Closing her eyes, she buried her face in the robe, and inhaled a deep breath. Jordana reveled in the scent teasing and tickling her nose. Hunger pangs made her feel light-headed. No wonder her stomach was growling. She hadn't had anything to eat since dinner last night, and she'd worked up an appetite between the sheets with Dante. She needed a hearty meal so she could complete her to-do list. She had to go grocery shopping, do laundry and make cookies for the bake sale at Matteo's school tomorrow. Add to that, she had acting class on Wednesday and needed to prepare for her dramatic scene presentation.

Jordana stalked through the room, cracked open the door and poked her head into the hall. Confident the coast was clear, she sprinted into the spare bedroom, and made a beeline for the closet. To wow Dante, she selected the purple chiffon halter dress he'd bought her at a boutique on Rodeo Drive, gold accessories and six-inch high heels. Jordana was excited about their lunch date, so anxious to see him butterflies swarmed her stomach. If he played his cards right, *she'd* be his dessert. Overcome with joy, she twirled around the room, giggling at the thought. Hearing her cell phone, she snatched it off the dresser, and put it to her ear. "Hello?"

"What's this nonsense about you getting married?"

Jordana choked on her tongue. *So much for the news not reaching Des Moines.* Though Helene couldn't see her, she dropped her gaze to the floor, and hung her head. Her mother's voice was quiet, filled with pain, and Jordana felt horrible for hurting her feelings. Driven by curiosity, she asked the question on the tip of her tongue. "Who told you?" she blurted out.

"You're not the one asking the questions, young lady. I am. Did you marry Dante Morretti in a secret wedding ceremony last Friday or not?"

"Yes, but—"

"But nothing!" she shouted. "Did you ever stop to think about your family? Obviously not, or you would have called to tell me, instead of leaving me to find out from the family I work for… "

Scared of going deaf, Jordana moved the phone away from her ear, listening quietly as her mom reamed her out in English *and* French. She'd seen Helene upset before, had even heard her swear a couple of times, but she'd never heard her this angry. She felt an overwhelming sense of sadness and guilt when her mother's voice cracked and she broke off speaking.

"Jordana, do you hate me? Do you resent me for being sick all these years?" she questioned, her tone thick with anguish. "Is that why you ran off and got married without telling me? Because you wanted to hurt me for being a bad mom?"

Her knees buckled, and she fell into the white reading chair in front of the window. Tears pricked her eyes, making her nose run and her vision blur. But Jordana spoke from the heart, determined to convey the love and admiration she had for her mother. Helene had single-handedly raised her and her brothers, and Jordana would never forget the sacrifices she'd made for them. "No, never, you're a fantastic mom and I wouldn't be the woman I am today if it wasn't for you. You're hardworking, strong and brave, and I love you more than anything."

Silence plagued the line, lasting so long Jordana feared her mom didn't believe her.

"What about Dante? Do you love him, or is this some sort of publicity stunt?"

The question surprised Jordana, caught her off guard,

and she suspected her mom had spoken to Waverly. Her best friend was the only person who knew about the marriage/custody scheme. Jordana wouldn't be surprised if her gossip-loving bestie had blabbed to her mom about her outrageous courthouse wedding days earlier. It wouldn't be the first time Waverly had let the cat out of the bag, and it probably wouldn't be the last. Driven by curiosity, she pressed the speaker button, and sent her best friend a text, posing the questions running through her mind. "What makes you think it's a publicity stunt?"

"You've told me numerous times that Dante's like a brother to you, so it was pretty easy to put two and two together." She added, "And besides, he's hardly your type. You prefer quiet guys, not arrogant playboys, and from what my friends at the bingo hall told me, Dante Morretti is a major player."

Mom, you're wrong, she argued, furiously shaking her head. *He's considerate and sensitive, generous and kind. I love him with all my heart, more than I've ever loved anyone, and if I wasn't scared of being hurt I'd tell him how I feel.*

"Is there anything *else* you want to tell me?"

"I'm not pregnant if that's what you're asking."

"Too bad!" Helene said. "I want some grandbabies and I'm not getting any younger!"

Jordana sidestepped the comment, pretending she didn't hear it, and apologized instead. "Mom, I'm sorry. I should have told you about the wedding, but I didn't know how."

"Baby girl, you can tell me anything. You know that. I won't always agree with your choices, but I love you and I want the best for you. I'll always be in your corner."

"Thanks, Mom."

"One more thing," she said quietly. "Did Dante give you the money to pay off my house? Is that why you married him?"

"Yes, he gave me the money, but no, that's not why we eloped. The foreclosure letter had nothing to do with it."

Helene released an audible sigh. "Thank God. I was worried you hooked up with Dante to help me out. I'm glad that's not the case."

"Don't worry, Mom, it's not." Noticing the time, she rose to her feet. "Mom, I'll call you later, okay? I haven't had breakfast yet, and I'm starving."

"Okay, baby girl. You go ahead. We'll have plenty of time to catch up when I get to LA."

Her mouth dropped, and a squeak escaped. "You're coming to LA? When? Why?"

"Because I'm anxious to meet my new grandson, and my handsome son-in-law."

"Mom, uh, now's not a good time."

"I know. You just got married, and you need to get settled in, right?"

"Yes," she said, relieved her mother understood her plight. "Exactly. Things have been crazy busy the last few weeks, and I need a moment to catch my breath."

"I figured as much. So, book my ticket for the end of July."

Jordana stared at the wall calendar, willing the numbers to change, but they didn't. Her mother was coming to LA and there wasn't a damn thing she could do about it.

Chapter 15

"Repeat the line, but this time narrow your eyes, fold your arms and raise your voice."

Jordana lowered the script to her side, slanted her head to the right as if studying the framed movie posters hanging on the cream walls inside the private screening room, and gave him a pointed look. "Come clean," she teased, hitching a hand to her hip. "You've been moonlighting as an acting coach for years, haven't you?"

Dante gave a hearty chuckle. They'd been hanging out for hours, trading laughs. He was having so much fun helping Jordana practice for her audition he'd forgotten about the paperwork waiting for him inside his home office. He was sitting in a cushy theater seat watching Jordana do her thing, marveling at how effervescent she was. And hot. Her curls tumbled around her face every time she laughed, her teal one-arm dress hugged her body in all of the places that mattered and her fruity perfume made him hanker for a mango as sweet and as juicy as her perfectly round ass.

Quit staring, cautioned his inner voice. *You're supposed to be helping, not lusting, so stop spacing out.*

They'd been married for three weeks, but Dante still couldn't believe they were husband and wife. Or that they'd made love every day since the dinner party. He left for work with a smile on his face, and he was so anxious to see her he often left the office early. Arriving home, his first stop used to be his office, but now he headed straight for the backyard. He'd find Jordana cooking in the outdoor kitchen or playing soccer with Matteo. Seeing them together warmed his heart.

Unfortunately, not everyone was thrilled about their union. Tavares had called yesterday, pissed that Dante had married Jordana despite his protests. His anger was understandable, justified even, and in spite of the hurtful things he'd said on the phone, Dante was looking forward to seeing him in July. He'd sit him down, buy him a beer, then explain why they'd tied the knot in a secret courthouse ceremony. If that failed, he'd buy him an expensive gift. Tavares loved the finer things in life, had a penchant for diamonds that could rival a Hollywood starlet, and the new Rolex watch would undoubtedly smooth things over.

Catching sight of the time on the wall clock, Dante wondered how his brother was faring out on the putting green. He'd planned to play golf with Markos and some out-of-town friends at the Beverly Hills Country Club, but when Waverly canceled on Jordana at the last minute, he'd volunteered to read lines with her and rescheduled with the Blanchett sisters. Though, he'd probably cancel on them again tomorrow. The twins were petulant divas who used their looks to get ahead—the complete opposite of Jordana—and he'd rather spend time with his family than accompany the twenty-something blondes to an industry event at the Playboy Mansion. "I'm not criticizing you, Jordana, so don't take this personally. I'm just offering a few helpful suggestions so you nail your audition tomorrow."

"How do you know so much about acting?"

Dante picked up his tumbler, and tasted his cognac. "Back in the day I dated a Kenyan girl who used to drag me around to casting calls, and I learned a few things about the business watching her jump through hoops trying to impress directors and producers."

"What happened to her? Did she make it in Hollywood?"

"Have you seen *With Just One Kiss*?"

Jordana squealed. "No way! Get out of here! *You* dated Ashante Starr? "

"I'll never tell," he said, flashing a boyish grin. "My lips are sealed."

"You're obviously an expert, so give me some more pointers."

Dante thought she was being sarcastic, teasing him about his past, but her eyes were bright with interest and she eagerly nodded as he spoke. "Jordana, you're doing great, but it could be better. You seem resigned, not angry. But if someone rear-ended me on my way to work, I'd be pissed."

"Maybe you're right."

"I'm definitely right," he said, with a wink and a nod.

"I'll try the scene again. I know I can do better."

"That's the spirit, Jordana. With that attitude you'll be a household name in no time."

Her face lit up, and his chest inflated with pride.

"Okay," she said, with a nervous smile. "Here goes."

Jordana read her lines, but this time she didn't hold back, and gave it her all. Blown away by her sudden transformation, Dante leaned forward in his chair. If he hadn't known her, he'd have thought she was an actress at the top of her game. She'd taken his advice, resulting in a powerful, emotional scene. Proud of her, he wanted to swoop her up in his arms and spin her around the room. Fear of looking sprung kept Dante in his chair and his hands in his lap.

His eyes took her in, raked over her body, noting every detail. Her dewy skin, moist, red lips, her Lord-have-mercy shape. Waking up that morning, their hands and legs were intertwined. Dante realized he didn't want to leave her side. He'd called his assistant, told her he'd be working from home and asked her to forward only important calls to his cell phone. Then he'd rolled over, pulled Jordana back into his arms and whispered sweet words in her ears.

Thinking about their morning quickie made his heart thump and sweat drench his body. Her loving had surpassed his wildest dreams. He'd never been intimate with someone who'd matched his drive, his intensity, and making love to her was the highlight of every day. Jordana was loud and expressive, passionate and eager. Her raunchy sex talk had spurred the most powerful orgasm he'd ever had. Hours later, he could still hear her voice in his ears, chanting his name, begging for more. Wanting her now, he imagined himself bending her over his chair, yanking off her panties and taking her from behind.

Harder than steel, his erection stabbed the zipper of his jeans, desperate for release. Dante heard his phone ring, suspected it was Markos calling to brag about his winning tee shot and took his cell out of the cup holder.

A sneer curled his lips, and a bitter taste filled his mouth. Lourdes was driving him crazy, a pain in the ass in Versace, and he had nothing to say to her. Deciding to let the call go to voice mail, he made a mental note to speak to Markos about their impending custody hearing.

"How was that? Any better?"

Dante glanced up from his phone, saw the hopeful expression on Jordana's face and pumped his fist in the air. "Baby, you killed it! That role is yours for the taking."

"Really? You think so?"

"Absolutely. Walk into that audition tomorrow as if you already have the part. That's how I approach every business deal. With confidence and boldness. It's the secret to my success, and my nothing-can-stop-me attitude has never failed me, not even when the chips were stacked against me and my boss counted me out."

Jordana strode across the room and sat down beside him.

"Knock 'em dead tomorrow. You're a Morretti now, and that's how we roll."

"I will," she promised. "I'm going to use all your tips and suggestions, as well."

Dante popped his shirt collar. "That *would* be the smart thing to do. I'm always right, and the sooner you realize it the happier you'll be."

"I just love your humility. It's so endearing," she said, her tone dripping with sarcasm.

They shared a laugh, gazed at each other affectionately, and Dante realized there was nowhere else in the world he'd rather be. He took her hand in his, held it tight, then gently caressed her fingers and wrist. It took every ounce of self-control not to crush his lips to her mouth and kiss her until he'd had his fill. If that was even possible. That morning in the shower proved he couldn't get enough of her, and if he had his way they'd spend the rest of the day in bed, living out their wildest fantasies. Dante could almost hear her moans now, envisioned the expression on her face as she climaxed and wondered if Jordana was in the mood, too. Sexually in sync, she never spurned his affections and often made the first move.

And Dante loved it. At the office, he gave orders, but at home Jordana called the shots. That suited him just fine. More persuasive than a politician, she'd convinced him to take a few days off work. Although his boss had cursed him out for missing his birthday bash at a posh nightclub, Dante didn't regret his decision. His family came first, and he never wanted his son to doubt his love.

Recalling the events of the past week brought a proud smile to his mouth. Matteo was thriving, and Dante had Jordana to thank. On Friday, they'd spent the morning exploring the Kids Discovery Center with Matteo, and in the afternoon sampled organic fruits and vegetables at the farmers' market. The following morning they'd gotten up early, packed the cooler with lunch and drove the thirty miles to Emma Wood State Beach to swim, fish and surf. It was the most fun he'd had in months, and he'd enjoyed goofing around with Matteo. Yesterday, to his son's delight, they'd "camped" in the backyard. They'd played board games, roasted hot dogs and marshmallows over the fire pit, and shared ghost stories. Once Matteo fell asleep, Dante had carried him inside to bed. He'd woken up with a big, fat smile on his face, anxious to go to school to tell his classmates about all of the cool things he'd done over the weekend.

"Thanks for helping me practice. I know how busy you are, and I really appreciate it."

"Don't tell me," he said smoothly, slowly licking his lips. "Show me."

She laughed, and the sound made him feel ten feet high, as if he'd just hit a hole in one.

"Jordana, I'll do anything for you. We're family now, and I'll always have your back."

For the second time in minutes, his cell rang and he glanced at it. Damn. Dante was sick of Lourdes blowing up his phone. But if he continued to ignore her calls she'd probably show up at his office again, and Dante didn't want his colleagues to know about his personal problems.

Putting the phone to his ear, he spoke through clenched teeth. "What. Do. You. Want?" he snapped, wishing she'd leave him the hell alone. Mindful of Jordana listening in, he chose his words carefully. Arguing with Lourdes always put him in a bad mood, and he didn't want his ex-wife to ruin his day. He'd made lunch reservations at The Swan Bistro, a cozy eatery in Orange County popular with reality stars, fashion icons and sports legends, and Dante was confident Jordana would love the romantic ambience and the vegan menu. "I told you to stop calling me and I meant it—"

"I miss Matteo. I haven't seen him in weeks, and I'm dying without him."

"You should have thought about *that* before your afternoon booze fest."

"And you're perfect, right?"

"No, but I'm not stupid enough to drive drunk."

"You're an asshole!"

"And you're a—" Dante saw Jordana cringe, and swallowed the insult on the tip of his tongue. "'Bye, Lourdes. Have a nice life."

"Dante, wait! I'm sorry. I shouldn't have said that."

He stared down at the phone, surprised by her apology. "What do you want?" he asked, unmoved by her woe-is-me act. "I'm busy, and I don't have the time to shoot the breeze."

"I—I—I need your help..." she stammered.

Her voice was so low Dante had to strain to hear what she was saying. He opened his mouth to speak, but Lourdes interrupted him, and he lost his train of thought.

"My attorney said if I want to get Matteo back I have to go to rehab, but I can't afford Destination Wellness," she explained. "I promise to repay you once I'm back on my feet."

"That's not my problem, so I suggest you ask your boyfriend, because I'm not an ATM."

"We broke up… I told him I wouldn't be moving to Boston, and he dumped me."

Dante wanted to shout for joy, but tempered his excitement. His biggest fear was losing his son, of not being around to watch him grow up. Learning his ex-wife's plans had fallen through was a huge weight off his shoulders.

"Dante, I know things have been tense between us since the divorce, but I'd like to start over. Let's put the past behind us, and work together to raise our son."

Disgusted, he snorted a laugh. Did Lourdes think he was stupid? Where was this benevolence and maturity when she was blackmailing him for half a million dollars? Her request was outrageous, the funniest thing he'd heard all day, and he refused to consider it. He didn't trust her, and he never would. "I have to go."

Dante hung up the phone, turned off the volume and returned it to the cup holder.

"How is Lourdes doing?"

"Who cares? I have better things to do with my time than worry about her."

"I understand that, Dante, but you share a son, and Matteo misses her desperately."

Filled with regret, he felt a pang of guilt. He couldn't bring himself to tell Jordana the truth, couldn't get his mouth to form the words. She wouldn't understand the choices he'd made, and he knew if he told Jordana what he'd done, she'd be disappointed in him. He didn't want to destroy their strong bond.

"When will Lourdes be out of rehab? Matteo is anxious to see her, and I bet she's—"

"Jordana, drop it. I don't want to talk about my ex or her screwed-up life."

"I hate when you do that."

Dantecocked an eyebrow. "Do what?"

"Shut me out."

"Jordana, calm down. You're overreacting and getting worked up over nothing."

"No, I'm not. Every time I ask you about Lourdes, or try to organize a visit for Matteo, you shut me down," she argued. "Don't worry. I get it. I know what's up. I'm good enough to screw, but I'm not good enough to confide in, right?"

Her bitter tone and hostile expression shocked him.

"Whoa," he said, slipping an arm around her shoulders, and pulling her in close. "Where did that come from? Is that what you think? That all I care about is sex?"

"Isn't it?"

"Of course not. We're a team, and I respect your opinion."

"Then act like it."

Dante opened his mouth, but couldn't find the words to say, and closed it.

"When I ask you about Lourdes, you treat me like a nuisance. It's frustrating."

"Baby, I'm sorry I made you feel that way. That was never my intention." He kissed her forehead, but her frown remained. "Please don't be mad. I have a great day planned for us, and a special surprise for you this evening."

A smile brightened her face, and Dante knew he was back in her good book.

"Are you taking me to the opera?" she asked.

Now it was his turn to frown. "I hate the opera."

"And I hate gangster rap but I didn't complain when you dragged me to that god-awful concert last Thursday. I got out of bed, made myself beautiful and pretended to enjoy myself even though I was bored out of my mind."

"Why don't you go see *Madame Butterfly* one day next week with Waverly?"

"Because you're my husband, and I want to go with you."

Grinning, he tightened his grip on her shoulder with

one hand, and cupped his ear with the other. "I missed that. Say it again. What did you call me?"

"My husband."

"I love the sound of that."

Jordana linked her arms around his neck, pulled him in close and licked her full, moist lips suggestively. "You smell good enough to eat, and I'm starving," she whispered, spraying kisses on his ears and along his jawline. "Are you thinking what I'm thinking?"

His body was—he had the erection to prove it—but his heart wasn't into it. Not now. Not after their heated conversation minutes earlier. Dante didn't want Jordana to think, not even for a second, that all he cared about was sex. Besides, there'd be plenty of time for makeup sex later, and he'd show her then how much he adored her. He would prove to her that she was the only woman he wanted in his bed, and in his life. "Baby, we can't," he said, determined to be the voice of reason. It was a challenge, because all he wanted to do was love her, but he remained strong. "We have one o'clock reservations at The Swan Bistro & Café—"

"Then we better make this quick." Her smile was cheeky, tinged with mischief, and her voice as seductive as sin. "Don't move."

"I wouldn't dream of it."

"Good, because I have a feeling you're going to like this."

Jordana dropped to her knees, freed his erection from his jeans and sucked it into her mouth. Chills overtook his body, causing his brain to short-circuit and his eyes to roll in the back of his head. Dante held his breath, marveling at all the tricks she could do with her teeth and tongue. Her technique gave him a rush, and made him feel like "the man." Scared he was going to explode, he ended their session before it had even started, pulled her into his arms, and kissed her. Her lips were sweet, addictive, flavored with tropical fruit. They'd had smoothies at breakfast, and he could taste traces of kiwi and guava on her tongue.

Sliding a hand under her dress, he was excited to feel her warm, bare skin. No panties, no bra, no problem. He cupped her breasts in his hands, caressed them, stroked them, felt her nipples harden as he mashed them together and sucked one, then the other nipple into his mouth.

"Do you have a condom?"

"No," he managed, between licks, "we finished the box this morning."

Jordana bit down on her bottom lip, looked pensive, suddenly unsure of herself.

"Why does it matter? We're happily married, and financially stable. We can fill this entire estate with kids if we want."

"Our relationship is complicated enough without adding a baby to the mix."

He made his nose twitch and his bottom lip tremble to pretend he was on the verge of tears. "You don't want to have my baby? Why not? It's Markos, isn't it? You're scared he'll be a bad influence on our little one, aren't you?"

Tossing her head back, she burst out laughing, filling the room with the infectious sound.

"You're ridiculous," she said, softly kissing his lips. "What am I going to do with you?"

"I'm sure you'll think of something." Dante winked. "The freakier the better."

Chapter 16

Jordana pulled into the Beverly Hills Preschool Academy parking lot at three o'clock, found an empty space in front of the chain-link fence and turned off the ignition. Lowering the radio, she took her cell phone out of her leather tote bag and typed in her password. She had three missed calls: one from her mom and two from Fallon. She hadn't booked her mom's plane ticket yet. She planned to hold off until she talked to Dante about Helene's visit first. She would give him the heads-up about her mom tonight at dinner.

Listening to Fallon's voice mail caused a scowl to pinch her cheeks. She was reluctant to call her agent back, had no desire to speak to her. On Saturday morning, when they'd met for tea at her favorite downtown café, Fallon had insinuated that she wasn't taking her acting career seriously, and three days later her words still stung. *It's not my fault I didn't get a starring role in Tyler Perry's new romantic comedy*, she thought, releasing a heavy sigh. *And I won't let Fallon make me feel guilty about it. Why did she have to bash me? Why couldn't she be supporting and encouraging like Dante?*

Troubled by her thoughts, she stared out the windshield. The sky was covered with thick, gray clouds, and the wind howled through the trees. These days, Jordana was busier than ever, but she loved her wonderful new life. Her days were filled with acting class, auditions and casting calls. Most days, after picking up Matteo from school they'd swing by The Brokerage Group for a short visit with Dante. He was always happy to see them, proudly showed them off to his colleagues and had healthy snacks waiting in his office for Matteo. Jordana felt herself changing as a person, improving as an actress, and she owed her newfound confidence to Dante. He read lines with her every night, was judicious with his praise and criticism, and unlike Fallon, championed her hopes and dreams.

Her cell phone rang, and after checking the number she put it to her ear. "Hey, Fallon, what's up?" she said with fake enthusiasm. "How's it going?"

"Good news! Renegade wants you to play his love interest in his music video!"

Jordana shrieked. "No way!"

"Yes way! I'm holding the contract in my hands as we speak—"

"Shut up, that's crazy. I never dreamed I'd get the part."

"You're in, girlfriend, and there's more," Fallon continued enthusiastically. "The director loves your natural, Bohemian look and wants you to audition for his romantic thriller."

Filled with excitement, Jordana danced around in her seat. "This must be my lucky day. It's about time because I've been busting my butt for years with no success."

"Well, that's about to change, because you've caught the eye of an up-and-coming director. I predict more great things in your future."

"Thanks, Fallon," she said, overcome with gratitude.

"The who's who of the music world will be at next Friday's shoot, so be your charming, lovable self, and network your ass off."

"Next Friday? Why the rush?"

"Renegade is leaving for his South American tour at the end of the month, and the record label wants to get the video out fast to generate more buzz about his concert dates. I just emailed the contract to you, so read it, sign it and FedEx it back to me ASAP."

"You don't have to tell me twice. I'm on it!"

"Good, this is the big break you've been waiting for, so don't mess it up. I'm counting on you, Jordana. Don't let me down."

Jordana ended the call, dropped her face in her hands and squealed. Finally! It wasn't a movie role, but it was a paying gig and she was thrilled about working with the rap superstar. She'd met Renegade at the audition, and to her surprise—and relief—he was nothing like his public persona. He was polite, soft-spoken, and in many ways reminded her of Dante.

At the thought of him a smile overwhelmed her lips. It was hard to believe their two-month anniversary was tomorrow. That morning, as they were cuddling in bed, he'd invited her to Tampa to attend the RaShawn Bishop Charity Golf Tournament, When she'd teasingly reminded him it was a guys-only trip, he'd tenderly stroked her face, and said, "My brothers are going to kick my ass for breaking the rules, but that's a beating I'll gladly take. I love being with you, and I sleep better when you're in my arms."

Then he'd kissed her, which resulted in them making love for the second time.

His feelings mirrored her own and long after he'd left for work, she'd lain in bed thinking about what he'd said. He believed in her, was her biggest supporter, and as she dialed his cell number her pulse sped up. Dante answered his cell on the third ring, and Jordana could tell by the noise in the background that he was outside.

"Hey, babe, what's up?" he greeted, his tone warm and jovial. "How was class today?"

"Dante, guess what! I'm going to be in Renegade's music video!"

"Is that right?"

"Yeah, and I'm so excited I feel like screaming at the top of my lungs!" Joy bubbled up inside her, and she laughed out loud. "I'm not the best dancer, but being in a music video sure beats doing another TV commercial."

"Jordana, don't do it. If you do, Hollywood will never take you seriously," he warned. "You'll be just another video girl with acting aspirations."

"Well, I'm not, and to be honest I don't care what anyone thinks."

"Not even me?"

"Dante, where is this coming from? We talked about this, and you said you were cool with it."

"Well, I'm not. I don't want my wife shaking her ass in music videos."

"Oh, my goodness!" she exclaimed, stunned by his admission. "You're jealous!"

"Jealous of a short, loudmouthed rapper? Hell no!"

"Then don't rain on my parade. Be happy for me."

"We'll talk about this later. I'm on-site, and I don't have time for idle chitchat."

"Fine," Jordana said tightly. She wished she could reach through the phone, and shake some sense into him, but she refused to let his negative energy ruin her moment, and spoke in a cheerful voice. "I'm making ribs for dinner, so don't be late."

"Get home safe, and tell Matteo I love him."

Click.

His behavior confused her, and left Jordana scratching her head. Her mind flashed back to that morning. Eight hours ago he'd rocked her world, given her the best sex of her life, and now he was tearing her down. *Don't do it... Hollywood will never take you seriously... I don't want my wife shaking her ass in music videos. What was up with that? Doesn't he trust me? Doesn't he know what this opportunity could do for my career? Does he even care?*

Remembering her conversation with Fallon, her smile returned. Jordana wanted to call everyone she knew—her family, Waverly, her former colleagues at LA Marketing who said she'd never make it in the business—to share her good news, but she saw the time on the dashboard clock and hustled inside to pick up Matteo. He was standing in the hallway, staring off into space, and he didn't respond when she called his name. "Hey, little man. How was your day?"

"Fine, I guess."

Jordana glanced inside the classroom, filled with books, colorful paintings and drawings. She wanted to speak privately with Ms. Papadopoulos, but parents were lined up in front of her desk. Making a mental note to email her later, Jordana picked up Matteo's backpack, slung it over her shoulder and took his hand. "How was school?" she asked, as they exited the building. "Did anything fun and exciting happen today?"

Matteo didn't answer, kicked a rock across the tree-lined street instead.

"Buddy, is everything okay?"

Head bent, shoulders hunched, he stared wordlessly at his Batman-themed runners.

Jordana stopped, crouched down so they were eye-to-eye, and spoke in a soft, soothing tone of voice. "What is it, Matteo? You can talk to me."

"I—I—I want my mommy," he stammered, his bottom

lip quivering uncontrollably. "Daddy said I'm a big boy, and big boys don't cry, but I miss her..."

Her heart broke for him. Using her fingertips, Jordana wiped the tears dribbling down his cheeks. "Do you want to call your mom when you get home?"

"Daddy said I can't. He said Mommy's sick, and I can't see her until she gets better."

Jordana took her cell phone out of the front pocket of her jean jacket, and punched in her password. "Let's call her now. I bet she misses you, too, and wants to hear your voice—"

"Mom!"

Matteo took off running, and Jordana scrambled to her feet, desperate to catch him before he ran out into the busy road. She turned around, just in time to see Matteo dive into Lourdes's open arms. The slender blonde stumbled in her high heels, and Jordana feared they'd topple over into the bushes. They stood there, hugging each other for what felt like hours, and when she heard Matteo giggle, tears pricked her own eyes. Jordana didn't want to hover, so she picked up his backpack, popped open the trunk and tossed it inside.

Hearing heels click-clack on the pavement, she turned to face Lourdes and smiled. They'd met a few times before, and on each occasion they'd chatted and laughed for hours about Matteo, their mutual love of vegan food, movies they wanted to see and celebrity gossip. "Hi, Lourdes. How have you been? It's great to see you."

She cocked an eyebrow. "It is?"

"Of course," she said, raising her cell phone in the air. "As a matter of fact, Matteo was just telling me how much he missed you, and we were going to give you a ring."

"You were?"

"Mommy, can you push me on the swings?" Matteo grabbed Lourdes's arm and dragged her across the field, chatting excitedly about his preschool graduation and karate class. Jordana hung back, didn't want to infringe on their private time together. They hadn't seen each other in weeks, and Matteo was so excited to see his mom he couldn't stop hugging and kissing her.

Remembering her earlier conversation with Fallon, she accessed the internet on her cell phone and checked her email. Jordana was so busy reading the music video contract she didn't realize Lourdes was standing beside her until she felt a hand touch her shoulder. Jordana glanced up, searched the playground for Matteo, and sighed in relief when she found him sitting in the sandbox. Children raced around the field, and frazzled-looking nannies held their backpacks in one hand and cell phones in the other.

"How is Matteo doing? Is he happy with you guys in Bel Air?"

"Matteo's doing great, but he misses you."

"He does?"

Jordana studied Lourdes closely, wondered if she'd fallen off the wagon again because her questions were ludicrous. Dark circles lined her eyes, suggesting she hadn't had a good night's sleep in weeks. But her yellow maxi dress was a perfect fit, and her hair, makeup and nails were immaculately done. "Yes, of course," she said slowly, giving her a puzzled look. "You're his mother, and he asks about you constantly. Why does that surprise you?"

"Because Dante said Matteo hates me."

"Matteo loves you, and now that you're out of rehab you can—"

"What makes you think I was in rehab?"

"You weren't?"

"I want to go, but I can't afford it," she said quietly. "I asked Dante for a loan so I could go to the Destination Wellness Ranch in Rancho Park, but he refused."

Her head throbbed, and it hurt to swallow. Realization

dawned, and for the second time that day Jordana was speechless. *Dante lied to me. He broke his promise.*

"If you weren't in rehab, then why haven't you returned any of Matteo's calls?"

"I lost my cell, but I gave Dante my new number weeks ago. He didn't give it to you?"

Jordana felt sick to her stomach, feared she was going to lose her lunch. Her mind raced, tried to make sense of what Lourdes was saying.

"Dante must have routed the calls from the home phone to his cell because every time I call he picks up. I know there's no way in hell he's home by four o'clock."

"Actually, he is. We take turns picking up Matteo from school, and he stopped working weekends so we can spend time together as a family."

"Wow, I'm impressed. He never listened to me when we were married. Still doesn't." Sadness filled her face, and seeped into her tone. "He told the principal to call the police if I ever show up at the school, and since I didn't want to embarrass Matteo I stayed away."

Jordana couldn't believe what she was hearing. Lourdes was lying. Had to be. Dante was a generous soul, a great father who'd never do anything to hurt his son, and she wasn't going to badmouth him. Still, she sympathized with Lourdes, and wanted to help.

"I woke up this morning and said, 'To hell with it. I'm going to go see my son,' and I'm glad I did. I love Matteo. I'll do whatever it takes to bring him back home."

Confused, and unsure of what to believe, Jordana told herself not to take sides. This wasn't her fight. Wasn't her issue. She was lucky to be living in Dante's mansion, was saving money like never before, and she remembered all of the kind, sweet things he'd done for her since their courthouse wedding. "What happened to your alimony settlement?" she asked, curious if what she'd heard about the former hairstylist was true. "Dante said you received a handsome check after the divorce—"

"I didn't blow it on drugs and booze if that's what you're asking."

"Then use that money to pay for rehab."

"I wish I could, but there's nothing left..."

Jordana offered a sympathetic ear. "What happened?"

"I paid down my debts, helped out my family and bought a high-end beauty salon in Orange County I'd hoped to manage." Lourdes stared out at the sky, her expression pensive, her shoulders hunched in defeat. "I trusted the wrong people, and less than a year later I was broke. To ease the pain I started drinking and...things just spiraled out of control."

Moved by her story, Jordana touched her shoulder and spoke from the heart.

"Matteo needs you, and if you don't get sober he'll grow up to resent you, or worse, hate you." Jordana paused, allowing time for her words to sink in. "Rehab isn't a quick fix, Lourdes. Neither is sobriety. It's a lifelong process, and you'll have to fight every day for the rest of your life to stay clean. But the rewards far outweigh the sacrifices."

"I don't know if I can do this alone. I have no one."

"Lourdes, that isn't true. You're not alone. You have me and Matteo, and you'll have the support of the counselors at the Destination Wellness Ranch, as well."

Car horns blared, school buses rumbled down the street, and boisterous conversation and laughter flowed on the breeze.

"You can do this," Jordana urged, willing her to be strong.

"You're right. I can. I want to do this for my son, and I won't let him down."

"No," she argued. "Don't do it for Matteo. Do it for yourself. You're worth it."

Lourdes hugged her. Jordana felt her body shudder,

heard her deep, racking sobs. She stroked her shoulders, and promised her everything would be okay. Talking to Lourdes dredged up bitter memories—memories from her past Jordana wished she could forget. She'd do anything to spare Matteo the pain she'd experienced as a child. Raised by an alcoholic mother and a distant father, she vividly remembered walking home from school every day, praying her parents weren't fighting, but they always were.

"Thanks for being a positive influence on my son, and for the talk."

Breaking free of her thoughts, Jordana nodded, and masked her grief with a smile.

"I know this sounds crazy, because we only met a few times, but I feel closer to you than my own sister. Chanelle doesn't understand what I'm going through. But you do."

"Unfortunately, I've had my fair share of struggles and setbacks. If not for a university counselor with a heart of gold, there's no telling where I'd be today."

"I know what I have to do." Her tone was strong, filled with determination and resolve. "I don't care what it takes. I'm going to get myself together and be a good mother to my son."

"That's the spirit, Lourdes!"

"It took losing custody of Matteo for me to see the errors of my ways, and I'll never, ever do anything to jeopardize our relationship. He's my heart, and I won't live without him."

"Can we go to McDonald's? Please? I promise to be good..."

Lourdes pulled away, wiped her face with the back of her hands and kissed the top of Matteo's head. "If it's okay with Jordana, it's okay with me."

Jordana was in a precarious situation, knew her decision could put her at odds with Dante, but she had to do what was right for Matteo. He needed his mother, and seeing him happy was all mattered. Nodding, she laughed when he squealed for joy.

"Swing me!" Matteo clasped their hands and took off running down the street. He flew high in the air, and dissolved into giggles when his feet touched the ground. "Again!"

"You're *just* like your father." Smiling, Jordana leaned over, and ruffled his curls. "You're not happy unless you're calling the shots. Go figure!"

Chapter 17

"Dad, guess what? Mom played with me at the park after school, and she's coming with us to the movies after dinner!"

Jordana entered the living room, saw Matteo jump into Dante's lap and smiled at the adorable twosome. On the drive home, all he could talk about was his mom. His face was bright, he gestured wildly with his hands as he spoke, and his voice was full of enthusiasm.

Chef Thierry was busy in the kitchen, likely preparing a feast fit for a king. Sniffing the air, Jordana smelled chocolate-chip cookies, and hankered for a sweet treat. Her mouth watered, but she made up her mind not to eat any junk food. She was taping a music video in three days, and if she wanted to keep up with the other dancers she had to hit the gym hard, not devour Chef Thierry's delicious baking.

"Slow down, Matteo. You're talking so fast I can't understand you."

He giggled. "Sorry, Dad, I'm excited!"

"I can see that." Dante dropped his cell phone on the couch, lowered the volume on the TV with the universal remote and stared at his son. "Now, tell me, li'l man, what's going on?"

"I'm going to the movies with Mom and Jordana tonight, and if I'm a good boy they promised to buy me popcorn, and chips and lots and lots of candy..."

Jordana didn't recall ever saying such a thing, but she saw the color drain from Dante's face and swallowed her objection. She was standing on the opposite side of the room, leaning comfortably against one of the reading chairs, but she could feel the anger radiating off Dante's body, saw it billowing in the air like smoke. Her first inclination was to leave, to flee the room before he unleashed his wrath, but Jordana didn't move. Why would she? She'd done nothing wrong, and she wouldn't let Dante make her feel guilty for doing the right thing. Lourdes's story—of Dante willfully and purposely shutting her out of Matteo's life—was shocking, and the more she spoke, the harder it was for Jordana to refute it. She hoped her intuition was wrong, that it was all one big misunderstanding. But had decided to reserve judgment until she talked to Dante.

"Matteo, go upstairs and change out of your school uniform," Dante instructed, rising to his feet. "After you clean your room I'll take you for a bike ride."

"You got it, Dad! Be back in a jiffy!"

But instead of going upstairs, Matteo skipped into the kitchen, climbed onto one of the stools at the breakfast bar and spoke in a hushed voice. Chef Thierry's big, booming laugh filled the room, and Jordana knew Matteo was on the hunt for cookies. And he'd get them. The staff spoiled him, his uncle, too, and Jordana didn't blame them. Like his father, he knew how to turn on the charm, and was impossible to resist.

"Jordana. In. My. Office. Now."

Before she could respond, Dante grabbed her forearm, and steered her down the hallway, his leather dress shoes pounding violently on the gleaming floors. She kept silent, willed herself not to argue even though she was annoyed by his sharp tone.

Dante led her into the darkened office, dropped her arm and slammed the door so hard Jordana was surprised it didn't fall off its hinges. It was a large space decorated in stone and steel furnishings, and the scrumptious white chairs and oversize couches invited rest and conversation. Her thoughts flashed back to the afternoon they'd made love on his desk, but she deleted the explicit images from her mind.

"What the hell is going on?" he demanded, posture stiff, arms crossed, his tone ice-cold.

"Lourdes showed up at Matteo's school today—"

"I heard. Why didn't Principal Caldwell call the cops? I gave her precise instructions to follow if Lourdes ever showed up, so why didn't she follow protocol?"

"Protocol?" she repeated, stunned by his words. "What are you talking about?"

"Isn't it obvious? Lourdes is a threat to herself, and more important, to my son."

Jordana opened her mouth, but broke off speaking when she heard her cell ring from inside her jacket pocket. Answering it would only acerbate the situation, so she ignored the untimely interruption. She suspected it was Fallon calling, and made a mental note to drop the contract off at her agent's Beverly Hills condo on the way to the theater. Jordana didn't feel like going to the movies, but she didn't want to disappoint Matteo. Speaking calmly, she said, "I know you and Lourdes have had an acrimonious relationship for years, but Matteo's her son, too, and she loves him just as much as you do."

"Jordana, stay out of it."

"For Matteo's sake, I have to speak. I can't keep quiet. What you're doing to Lourdes is mean and vindictive and—"

"Justified!" he shouted, his strident tone piercing her eardrum. "She's an alcoholic, and I don't want her anywhere near my son. Do you hear me?"

Her face must have showed her disappointment, her outrage, because he dismissed her with a flick of his hand, and paced the length of the room, mumbling under his breath.

"Forget it. I don't even know why I'm wasting my breath. You're not a parent. You wouldn't understand the stress I'm under."

"You're right. I don't understand," she shot back. "I don't understand how you can be so cruel to the woman who gave you a beautiful, healthy son."

"You don't know the hell she's put me through."

"Quit punishing Lourdes for the mistakes of the past, and help her to be a better mother, because every time you hurt her, you're inevitably hurting Matteo. Don't you see that?"

His eyes iced over, clouded with disgust.

"Dante, she's ready to change, and I want to help her."

"Leave it alone. There's nothing you can do."

At war, her head and heart clashed, but Jordana knew she had to tell Dante the truth, and let the chips fall where they may. "I already did," she said, wishing she wasn't shaking like a leaf. "I wrote Lourdes a check to cover her stay at Destination Wellness. She starts treatment on Monday."

Dante stopped pacing, his gaze darker than his jet-black suit. "You did what?"

It wasn't a rhetorical question—the scowl, twisting of his lips, confirmed he'd heard what she said—so she kept quiet.

"You had no right to give Lourdes my money."

"Excuse me?" she snapped, folding her arms across her chest. "*Your* money?"

"That's right. My money. You work for me, not her."

Pain stabbed her heart. There it was. The truth. Finally, after weeks of playing house with Dante, she now knew where she stood. They would never have a real marriage, never have the kind of relationship she'd always longed for. One founded on unconditional love, mutual respect and trust. In his eyes, she was just another member of his staff, another employee to do his bidding. If she stepped out of line, she'd surely be fired.

"You can't dictate how I spend my weekly allowance—"

"I can, and I will. This is my house, and you'll live by my rules."

The knot in her chest threatened to kill her dead, but she spoke in a quiet tone that veiled the anger bubbling in her veins. "My apologies." Her inner mean girl rose to the surface and a verbal bitch slap fell from her mouth. "I thought *my* money was for me to spend as I please. My bad. The next time I sign a prenuptial agreement I'll make sure I read the fine print."

"Lourdes conned you out of thirty grand, but you're too blind to see it."

"Do you hear yourself? Do you hear how cold you sound?"

"I don't care. She can fool you, but she damn sure isn't fooling me."

"Stop! Enough already!" she shouted, giving voice to her anger. Who did Dante think he was? How dare he speak to her with disdain and disrespect. "This isn't about Lourdes. This is about you being a control freak! That's why you have two high-powered jobs, why you work insane hours and why you're mad Renegade wants me to be in his music video. You're not happy unless you're calling the shots and telling everyone else what to do. But I won't let you or anyone else control me. I'm my own boss, my own woman, and you can't run my life."

The desk phone rang, drawing her gaze across the room. Jordana hoped Dante answered it, so she could leave him *and* his bad attitude in her dust, but he didn't.

"What do you want from me?"

"Nothing, because if you can treat the mother of your child like crap there's no telling what you'll do to me. After all, I'm just the hired help."

Surprise covered his face, and sadness flickered in his eyes. He looked at her for a long, terse moment. He didn't speak. Just stared, as if they were strangers meeting for the first time.

"Get out, and don't come back."

"With pleasure," she shot back.

Dante pointed at the office door. "I want you out of my estate *now*."

"I'm not going anywhere. I promised Matteo I'd take him to the movies, and unlike you, I *always* keep my word." Calmly, despite her trembling legs, she opened the door and fled the room. Jordana wanted to run, to get as far away from Dante as she could, but she didn't have the strength it required. She felt drained, depleted, as if she'd gone twelve rounds with a champion boxer, and it took all her strength to climb the staircase. Her vision was blurry, but she strode down the hall into her bedroom and collapsed against the door. Only then, when Jordana was alone in the darkness, did she let the tears flow.

Chapter 18

Dante heard the doorbell chime, suspected it was Markos banging on his door like a deranged lunatic, but he didn't get up from his chair. Kept his feet propped up on the coffee table, Corona in hand, Italian rap music blaring on the stereo. His brother was doing his daily rounds, checking up on him, but Dante wasn't in the mood for another lecture. Not today. Not after everything he'd been through since Jordana left.

Dante dragged a hand down the length of his face and massaged the back of his neck. He was beat, dog tired, and would do anything for a good night's sleep. It had been the longest week of his life, and the more Markos badgered him about reuniting with Jordana, the guiltier he felt about kicking her out. She was the woman he'd been waiting his whole life for, without a doubt the smartest, most beautiful female he'd ever seen, and he'd tossed her out of his house. Jordana wasn't afraid to tell him the truth, even though others were, and he respected her for that. What he didn't respect was her joining forces with Lourdes. They were supposed to be a team. Best friends. Husband and wife. But a week after their breakup he still couldn't understand why she'd betrayed him.

The banging grew louder.

"Leave me alone," he grumbled. "Worry about your own damn life for once."

Glancing at his watch, he wondered why Markos was on his doorstep instead of annihilating opposing counsel in court. But he thanked his lucky stars his brother had lost his spare key months earlier, or he'd have no choice but to listen to his god-awful advice. Markos showed up at his estate every night, claiming he was worried about him, but Dante was tired of his impromptu visits, his know-it-all attitude and his incessant questions about Jordana.

For that reason, he ignored the chiming doorbell. Jordana was gone, she wasn't coming back, and that was that. Yesterday, within seconds of arriving, Markos implored him to call her, begged him to make things right, but Dante refused. Hell no. Jordana should be calling *him*. He wasn't the one who'd betrayed her, who'd plotted and schemed with her ex behind her back, and it would be a cold day in hell before he apologized. Forget that. They were over, and the sooner his annoying, meddlesome brother realized it, the better. Thinking about his conversation with Markos last night while they played Xbox in the media room caused his blood to boil.

"Bro, I'm worried about you," he'd said, his expression and his tone filled with concern. "You're exhibiting all the classic signs of depression. You're not sleeping—"

"I'm amped up about our guys trip to Tampa this weekend."

"You're not eating—"

"I'm doing a cleanse," he'd answered with a dismissive shrug. "No biggie."

"And you quit your job—"

"So I can spend more time with Matteo. Sue me for wanting to be a better dad!"

Dante brought the bottle to his lips, and took a swig of his Corona, thinking about the lies he'd told his brother last night. He didn't tell Markos the truth—that his argument with Jordana had been the driving force behind his decision to leave The Brokerage Group—and he didn't plan to. He'd submitted his resignation letter three days ago, and every time he remembered Mr. Smirnov's reaction, how he'd cursed and raged in Russian, Dante knew he'd made the right decision. Now he could devote all of his time and energy to taking Morretti Realty to the next level, and building friendships with influential businessmen such as Mr. Quan. In September he planned to visit the Chinese billionaire in Hong Kong, and this time he was taking Matteo.

I wish Jordana could come, but fat chance of that ever happening, he thought sourly, downing the rest of his drink. *She hates me, and I don't blame her. I messed up, and I'll never forgive myself for losing the only woman I've ever truly loved.*

"Dad, get up. Jordana's at the door, and you have to let her in."

Snapping to attention, Dante shook off his thoughts, and sprung to his feet. Matteo was standing in the hallway, chocolate stains covering his mouth and hands, and he wore an innocent smile. He was supposed to be packing for his weekend visit to his aunt Chanelle's house, but it was obvious he was helping himself to the sweets in the pantry. "Matteo, are you sure?

His head bobbed. "Yes. I peeked out the window, and she waved at me."

Dante sighed in relief. Couldn't believe his good luck. Deep down, he wanted Jordana back, home where she belonged, and this time when they talked he wasn't going to lose his temper. He was going to listen, and he promised himself he'd be calm and respectful, no matter what.

"I'm glad Jordana's home," Matteo said, licking his fingertips. "I missed her cooking, her bedtime stories and playing soccer with her. It's so much fun. I always win!"

I miss her, too, li'l man, and I'll never hurt her again.

Dante raked a hand through his hair and straightened his clothes. He wished he was wearing something nicer than an old Lakers T-shirt, basketball shorts and Nike sandals, but he didn't have time to change. Marching down the hallway with Matteo at his side, he hoped Jordana was still waiting on the doorstep, and broke into a light jog.

Reaching the foyer, Dante blew out a deep breath. He unlocked the front door, and slowly opened it, taking his time. No sense looking eager. The last thing he wanted was for Jordana to think he'd been sitting in the house for the past week waiting anxiously for her return—even though he had. Dante talked a good game, convinced himself, and Markos, that their breakup was for the best. But the truth was he loved Jordana, always had and always would. He was broken without her.

He expected to see Jordana standing on the doorstep, carrying the Louis Vuitton suitcases she'd left with days earlier, but was shocked to find a stocky Spanish man with a moustache and a slender woman with oversize sunglasses and high cheekbones. She was an older, darker-skinned version of Jordana with the same wild unruly hair, and Dante instantly knew who she was. Shit! What were her parents doing in LA? Did they know he'd kicked her out? Was her dad there to beat him up for hurting his only daughter?

"We're Jordana's parents, Fernán Batista and Helene Sharpe. You must be Dante."

He coughed, to clear the lump in his throat, and nodded. "Yes. Welcome."

"Hi," Matteo said brightly, extending a chocolate-stained hand. "I'm Matteo."

The couple shared a knowing smile, and shook his son's small gooey hand.

"You're Jordana's mom? That means you can cook."

Helene wore an amused expression. "Who told you?"

"Jordana said you used to make her chocolate-chip waffles when she was a little girl, and they're my favorite. Can you make me some, too?"

"Matteo, you're not hungry. You had cereal less than an hour ago."

"Cereal, Dad, not waffles," he said, stressing his words. "They're different."

"I'd love to cook for you. It would be my pleasure." Helene turned to Fernán, and shoved her purse into his arms. "Be a dear and take my things to my room. I'm going to make breakfast with my adorable new grandson."

"Jordana isn't home," Dante blurted out.

Fernán gave a curt nod. "That's fine. We'll wait."

You could end up waiting the rest of your lives, he thought sourly.

"Waffle time!"

Off Matteo went, skipping into the kitchen with Helene, leaving Dante alone in the foyer with Jordana's menacing-looking father.

"We need to talk," Fernán barked, slamming the front door. "Follow me."

Follow you? But this is my *house!*

"Sir, let me show you to the guest cottage first."

"No, you're going to tell me where my daughter is, and you're going to do it now."

His mind made up, Fernán strode into the living room,

sat down in Dante's favorite chair and gestured for him to have a seat.

Feeling like a delinquent student in trouble with the principal, he sat down on the couch. Dante tried to appear cool, unfazed, but the murderous expression on Fernán's face made him uneasy. According to Jordana, her dad was an athletic recruiter, but the man looked like a hired assassin. Dante wondered if the recruiter job was just a cover to hide his true profession.

"I'm waiting," he prompted, cracking his knuckles.

"Sir, like I said earlier, Jordana's not here."

"Why not?"

"We had a fight, and she left. I haven't seen or talked to her since."

"What happened? Helene says you're a good guy who's always looked out for our daughter, so none of this makes sense." He furrowed his thick eyebrows, as if perplexed, and leaned forward in his chair. "You didn't do anything stupid like cheat on her, did you?"

"No, never."

Lines wrinkled his forehead. "You're sure? I did an online search on you and your family, and it seems you Moretti boys like chasing tail. Any truth to that?"

"I haven't looked at another woman since we got married, and I won't. Jordana is the only one for me, and if I can't have her, I don't want anyone."

"Then what are you doing to get her back?"

Dante hung his head. The question made him feel low, made him realize how stupid he'd been. He hadn't called her because he was too proud to make the first move, but Jordana was worth fighting for. He wanted to make things right while he still had the chance. It wasn't too late. Not all was lost. He swiped his cell phone off the couch, and punched in Jordana's number. The call went to voice mail. No surprise. She was angry at him for losing his temper, and Dante didn't blame her. Remembering the things he'd said made him cringe.

"Helene raised Jordana to be a strong, independent woman, and sometimes I think she did too good a job," Fernán confessed. "Jordana's never confided in me about her problems, and it's been a bone of contention between us for years. I'm her father, but if my professor friend at Drake University didn't call and tell me about her accident, I never would have known she had been hospitalized or expelled from school."

Bowled over by the news, Dante sank back in his chair. Questions shot out of his mouth, fast and furious. "What accident? What happened? Why was Jordana kicked out of school?"

"She never told you?"

"Never told me what?"

Fernán coughed into his fist. "It's not my place to say."

"Sir, please? I'm lost, and I could use your insight right now."

His expression was grim, but after several seconds of quiet deliberation he slowly nodded. "Helene loves Jordana and her brothers, Carlito and Raymon, more than anything, but she's struggled with substance abuse their entire lives. After years of fighting with her to get help, I checked out of the relationship. I wasn't there for Jordana when she needed me most, and by the time she got to college she had no use for me."

All of the pieces of the puzzle fit, and suddenly everything made sense. Her burning desire to help Lourdes, why she'd paid for his ex-wife to go to rehab, why she preached forgiveness and acceptance. As a child she'd been caught in the middle of her parents' tumultuous relationship, and wanted to prevent the same thing from happening to Matteo.

"I've held a grudge against Helene for years. I felt her

poor choices influenced Jordana, but when she called me last night and told me our baby girl had eloped, it broke my heart."

Looking back, Dante realized his stubborn, know-it-all attitude had been a problem in their relationship from the beginning. He had all the answers—or so he'd foolishly thought—and had never considered her words of wisdom. They played in his mind now, piercing his heart, and wounding him afresh. *I see myself in Lourdes… Everyone deserves a second chance… Help her to be a better mom.* In that moment, Dante loved Jordana more than he'd ever loved anyone and declared in his heart to win her back. He had to talk to her. Now. Before it was too late and he lost her forever. He had to do something. Had to act. Couldn't sit around twiddling his thumbs anymore, but was out of ideas.

"I need to apologize to Jordana for not being a good father, and beg for her forgiveness."

"That makes two of us, Mr. Batista."

"Call me Fernán. I like you, son, and I think you're good for my daughter."

"No," he corrected. "It's the other way around. Your daughter's good for *me*. She's given me a whole new outlook on life, and made me a better man and father, and for that I'm eternally grateful."

"Do you have any idea where my daughter could be? We've called her friends, and even her old boss at LA Marketing, but no one's seen her, and she isn't answering her cell phone."

Hearing laughter coming from the kitchen, Dante glanced over his shoulder. Ms. Sharpe was feeding Matteo chocolate chips, gazing lovingly at him, as if he was the only child in the world who mattered. His son had charmed Jordana's mother, no doubt showered her with hugs and kisses and smiles, and now Helene was eating out of the palm of his hand.

Dante bolted upright in his seat. *That's it!* Matteo was the answer to his problems. Mad at himself for not thinking of it sooner, he formulated a winning plan in his mind, guaranteed to work. It was time to get back on his A game, and not a moment too soon. Excitement must have shown on his face because Fernán clapped him on the shoulder, and asked, "What is it?"

"I know what to do to bring Jordana home."

"You do? Then what are we waiting for?"

"Sir, I'll have to lie to pull this off. What I'm about to do is sneaky and underhanded and could backfire in my face, so I understand if you don't want any part of it."

"Do whatever it takes to bring my daughter home."

The men shook hands, but the gesture did nothing to assuage Dante's guilt. He hoped Jordana would find it in her heart to forgive him for what he was about to do. Unfortunately, he had no choice. No other options. He had to bring his baby home, and the sooner the better. He'd never understood the power of true love until he'd met Jordana, and he'd move heaven and earth to win her back. He didn't have any doubts. Not one. She was his soul mate, the woman of his dreams, and he was proud to call her his wife.

Blowing out a deep breath, Dante rose to his feet, snatched the cordless phone off the cradle and strode into the kitchen to coach his son.

Chapter 19

Jordana was flying down the interstate, driving twenty miles over the posted speed limit, but it felt as if her Bentley was moving at a snail's pace. Sweat drenched her skin, and her pulse clapped in her ears like thunder. "God, please, let him be okay," she prayed, fighting back tears. "Please don't let anything happen to Matteo."

Punching the gas pedal with her snakeskin pumps, she willed the Bentley to go faster, and weaved expertly through midday traffic. Thoughts of Matteo, the darling little boy she loved more than life itself, bombarded her mind, and a suffocating knot burned inside her chest. "Hang on, li'l man. I'm on my way."

Jordana relived the past thirty minutes, replayed every detail in her mind. She was on the set of Renegade's music video saying goodbye to the hardworking cast and crew when Dante's home number appeared on her cell phone.

Exiting the studio loft, only miles from Venice Beach, she'd pressed Talk, put the phone to her ear and, despite the butterflies in her stomach, spoke in a carefree tone, as if she was on top of the world. Disappointment and happiness had flooded her heart in equal measures, but before Jordana could ask Matteo how he was doing he'd burst into tears.

Her cell phone chimed from the center console, cueing Jordana she had a new text message, but she paid it no mind. Her mom and Waverly had been blowing up her phone all day, but she'd let their calls go straight to voice mail. Every time she thought about Dante her heart ached, and she didn't want her friends and family to know she was shaken up over the loss of her one true love.

Her thoughts returned to last Wednesday. The morning after their argument she'd dropped Matteo off at school, checked into The Westin and crawled into bed, wishing she could go back in time and undo the mess she'd made of her relationship. She'd been at the hotel ever since, but had been searching the classifieds daily for affordable housing. Returning to Dante's estate was out of the question, but she wouldn't abandon Matteo. She'd take care of him until Lourdes returned from rehab, then relinquish the caregiver role to his bickering parents.

Jordana turned left on Bel Air Road. The estate came into sight, and memories of brighter days warmed her heart. To her relief, the security gate was wide open. She sped through it, up the driveway, and parked in front of the fountain. Desperate to reach Matteo, she unbuckled her seat belt, jumped out of the car and raced inside.

"Matteo, baby, I'm here. Where are you?" she called, marching through the main floor.

Jordana listened for a moment, heard nothing and headed upstairs. She opened Matteo's bedroom door, and stopped dead in her tracks. Dante. He was standing beside the window, and a broad smile was on his lips. She stared right at him, noted he looked just as handsome in sportswear as he did in designer threads. His tousled locks and the dark stubble along his jawline increased his sex appeal. But she was at the estate to check up on Matteo, not jump his bones, so she searched the spacious sun-filled room for the precocious preschooler. "Where's Matteo? Is he okay?"

"Of course. He's fine."

"He said he fell down the staircase and broke his leg."

"That's not true…"

Jordana folded her arms. She sensed he was lying to her, saying what he thought she wanted to hear, but she wasn't leaving until she saw Matteo for herself and checked him out from head to toe. Jordana looked in the closet, under the bed and in the laundry basket, but Matteo wasn't in any of his favorite hiding spots. *What the hell?* He'd called her thirty minutes earlier, crying hysterically, begging her to come home, and now he was nowhere to be found.

Ignoring Dante, she stepped past him, and glanced out the window. A gasp fell from her mouth. Her parents were in the backyard with Matteo, and it was quite the sight. Matteo doing fancy footwork with the soccer ball, her dad hopping around in front of the net trying to prevent the goal, her mom waving pink pom-poms wildly in the air.

"M-my parents are here," she stammered.

"I'm glad you invited them."

"I didn't. My mom invited herself."

Dante laughed, but Jordana didn't find anything funny about her parents being in LA.

"What are they doing here? My mom wanted to come visit at the end of the month, but I convinced her to come for Christmas and she never once mentioned bringing Fernán."

"Your mom told your dad we eloped, and he jumped on the first flight to LA."

Jordana widened her eyes. "I can't believe it. Matteo tricked me, and I fell for it hook, line and sinker."

"I asked him to call you."

"Why?"

"Because we need to talk, and I knew you'd come home if you thought Matteo was hurt."

"Forget it. I'm tired, and I'm not in the mood for another lecture about spending *your* money, following the rules in *your* house and staying away from *your* son." Jordana realized she was yelling and lowered her voice. "The things you said on Wednesday deeply hurt me."

"Jordana, I'm sorry. I was upset, and I said a lot of things I didn't mean. You've been my rock the last few months, and if not for you I never would have won custody of Matteo, or resigned from the Brokerage Group. Now we can spend more time together as a family."

Jordana was shocked by his confession, and secretly pleased, but she didn't share her thoughts.

He took her hand in his, and her heart melted. Jordana wanted to pull away, to tell him they were over for good, but her mouth couldn't form the words. His touch was welcome, wanted, and when he sat on the bed and took her into his arms, she felt loved.

"I was angry, and I took my frustrations out on you…"

Jordana listened, didn't interrupt, but his confession made her feel worse, not better. What happened the next time he got mad at her? Would he insult her, and kick her out of the house again?

"You're nothing like Lourdes, and—"

"Dante, you're wrong. I *was* her. I partied hard when I was in college, and it cost me everything." His eyes were filled with concern, and his tender caress along her shoulders gave Jordana the strength to finally open up to him about her past. Her voice wobbled, shook with emotion, but she conquered her nerves, and bared her soul. She told Dante about her childhood, the pain of watching her mother struggle with substance abuse and her stressful years at Drake University. "I didn't realize I had a drinking problem until I crashed my car into the Student Union building one night after a wild frat party."

"You could have been injured."

"Something worse happened. I was expelled, and ordered to pay the damages. I hit rock bottom that night, and promised myself I'd never touch alcohol again. I'm proud to say I haven't, and whenever I crave alcohol I keep myself busy by doing something fun like surfing, fishing or hiking. You wanted to know why I love the great outdoors, and now you know why."

"We've been friends for two years, but you never said anything. Why not?"

"Because I was embarrassed, and I was scared if I told you the truth you'd want nothing to do with me," she confessed. "It's happened before, and I didn't want to take the chance."

"Jordana, quit beating yourself up. Everyone's done things they regret. Even me."

"Then why are you so hard on people? Why do you demand perfection when it's impossible to achieve?"

"Because that's the Morretti way. My father raised me and my brothers to be the best, no matter the cost. It's a philosophy I've always lived by, and it governs everything I do."

"But it's stressful trying to live up to other people's expectations."

"You don't have to. The only person who matters is me!"

His boyish smile made her laugh, and lightened the tense mood.

"I wish you had told me about your past sooner."

"Would it have mattered?"

"Absolutely. If I'd known I wouldn't have been such an ass on Wednesday night."

"Luckily I was able to get myself together without going to rehab, but not everyone with a drinking problem is strong enough to quit cold turkey," she explained, recalling a conversation she'd had with her mom's sober coach years earlier. "Lourdes wants to get better, and I feel compelled to help her, so please don't fight me on this anymore."

A dark shadow passed across his face, caused his body to tense, and she could tell he was angry, struggling to control his temper. She wondered for the umpteenth time what his ex-wife had done to irretrievably damage their relationship. "Did Lourdes cheat on you while you were married? Is that why you're holding a grudge against her? Because she broke your heart?"

"Jordana, I don't want to talk about it."

"So we can talk about my past, but we can't talk about yours? How is that fair?"

"I don't want to argue."

"Then open up to me. Tell me why you're so angry at Lourdes—"

"Because she set me up. That's why. She went to the club that night with the sole purpose of sleeping with me and getting pregnant, and I fell right into her deceitful trap."

"Are you sure? How do you know this? It could be nothing but malicious gossip."

"It's not. The words came straight from her mouth." He turned away from her, lowered his head and rubbed at his eyes. "I found out Lourdes was having an affair with my business rival Zachary Montenegro shortly before we separated. The day she filed for divorce, I tracked her down to the douche bag's Malibu mansion. I begged her to give me my son, and she laughed in my face. I know it was years ago, but every time I look at her I remember that fateful night. I despise her for what she did, and I want to hurt her the same way she hurt me."

"Dante, for Matteo's sake you have to put the past behind you, and move on. You have to stop punishing Lourdes for her mistakes."

Silence fell between them, and after a long moment Dante spoke.

"I want to, but I don't know if I can."

"Of course you can," Jordana insisted, tenderly stroking his face. "You're a Morretti, and Morrettis can do anything they put their minds to, remember?"

"I'll try."

Faking a scowl, she playfully punched his shoulder. "You better, or that's your ass!"

Dante erupted in laughter, and the sound of his hearty chuckle warmed her all over.

"Let's make a deal," he proposed. "I'll visit Lourdes tomorrow in rehab to discuss a visitation schedule for Matteo if you promise to spend some one-on-one time with your dad tonight. He's anxious to speak to you, and I promised I'd put in a good word for him."

Jordana gave his suggestion some thought. She hadn't spoken to her father since they argued at her brother's wedding, but she was ready to make amends. "I'll do it."

"How did the video shoot go?"

"I'm surprised you remembered.

"Are you kidding me? It's all I could think about. Last night I had a nightmare that you eloped with Renegade, and had a bunch of gold chain–wearing babies!"

Jordana laughed. "We wrapped up the shoot this afternoon, and the video for 'On Fleek' is sexy, sultry and hot!" she said, fanning her face with her hands to emphasize her point. "I'm proud of the work we did, and I'm confident it's going to be a hit."

"Is there a kissing scene?"

"Yes, but I'm not in it. His fiancée is!"

"I have something for you."

Dante reached into his pocket, took out her wedding ring and slipped it back on her finger. Jordana beamed. A week ago, she'd taken it off and put it back in the Cartier box, but she was thrilled to be wearing the gorgeous diamond again and loved seeing it on her left hand.

"I meant what I said on our wedding day, Jordana."

"Seriously? Even though it was all for show? You actually meant your vows?"

"With all my heart. You're the only woman for me, and nothing would make me happier than spending the rest of my life with you. I love you, Jordana, and so does Matteo. You're my life, my everything, and there's no place I'd rather be than right here with you."

Overcome with joy, Jordana felt as if her heart would burst with happiness. An overwhelming sense of peace showered over her, and she knew deep inside there'd never be another man for her. He was her one true love, the man she'd been waiting for her entire life. "I love you, too, Dante, more than words can express, and I'm proud to be your wife."

Mischief gleamed in his eyes. "Don't tell me. Show me."

And she did. Cupping his face in her hands, she pressed her lips to the tip of his nose, each cheek and finally his mouth. Her kiss was slow, thoughtful, full of warmth and tenderness. Their relationship was explosive and intense, but Jordana wouldn't have it any other way. They were destined to be together, and no one else would ever do.

"I love you so much it scares me sometimes," he said, pausing to stare deep into her eyes.

"Baby, you have nothing to worry about. I'm not going anywhere. I'm yours for life."

Caressing his smooth, soft skin with her fingertips, she playfully nibbled at the corners of his lips. He played in her hair, twirled curls around his fingers, all the while whispering words of love and admiration in her ears. For as long as Jordana lived, she'd never forget this moment, would never forget how cherished Dante made her feel. And when he scooped her up in his arms and set off for the master bedroom, Jordana melted against him, deeply grateful that she finally had the life she'd always dreamed of.

* * * * *

SPECIAL EXCERPT FROM

HARLEQUIN®

Elite boutique owner Autumn Dupree is a realist when it comes to relationships. Until nightclub owner Ajay Reed arouses a passion she never knew existed…

*Read on for a sneak peek at FALLING FOR AUTUMN, the next exciting installment of Sherelle Green's **BARE SOPHISTICATION** series!*

"What am I going to do about this?" she said aloud to the empty alley.

"For starters, how about you avoid walking out into dark alleys by yourself."

Her head flew to the door she had just exited and her eyes collided with his. No man had a right to look that sexy. Ajay had on a black shirt and dark jeans. But instead of his usual footwear, he had on a pair of black shoes. The lines of his fade and goatee were so clean, there was no doubt that he'd just gotten a haircut. He took a few steps closer to her until he was standing under the same light she was.

"Why did you come out here?"

"I needed to breathe."

He studied her eyes, and it took all her energy to stand there and not fidget under his intense gaze. Her breathing was scattered and her heart felt as if it had actually skipped a beat.

HKMREXP0316

"Why were you flirting with Luke? I thought you didn't like him like that."

"I don't. But..." Her voice trailed off when she realized she had been about to tell him the truth.

"But what?"

She couldn't believe she was really contemplating telling him. "He told me that the longer he hugged me, the more upset you would get."

"He said that?"

"Yes. He also told me that the minute he kissed my cheek, the vein in your neck would pop. Then he told me to see what would happen if I placed my arm on his shoulder."

He squinted in curiosity. "So, were you trying to get a rise out of me to please him...or yourself?"

She swallowed the lump in her throat as her gaze bounced from his eyes to his lips. "I think it was a little bit of both. It was his birthday, so I was being polite. But I also wanted to see how you would react."

His eyes dropped to her lips. "You don't want to play games with a man like me, Autumn."

HKMREXP0316